LIVES AND LOVES

The Stories of Rowland Davis

ROWLAND DAVIS

Edited by Margot Norris

PublishAmerica
Baltimore

PublishAmerica has allowed this work to remain exactly as the author intended, verbatim, without editorial input.

Softcover 9781629070995
PUBLISHED BY PUBLISHAMERICA, LLLP
www.publishamerica.com
Baltimore

Printed in the United States of America

ABOUT THE AUTHOR

Rowland Hallowell Davis was born in Boston, Massachusetts on December 8, 1933 to Hallowell Davis and Pauline Allen Davis. He was the youngest of three siblings. His brother, Allen Young Davis, was eight years his senior, and his sister, Anne Hessey, was seven years older. Both have predeceased him.

Rowland lived in Belmont, Massachusetts for the first eight years of his life. During this time his father taught at Harvard and conducted research on the physiology of hearing. Hallowell Davis was the first person in the United States to have his brain scanned by an EEG device. He was awarded the National Medal of Science by President Gerald Ford in 1975. Rowand's mother committed suicide when he was eight years old and he was sent to live with his aunt and uncle, Esther Fisher Brown and Ralph Brown, who acted as parents for that year. He attended fourth grade at Staten Island Country Day school and then returned to Concord, Massachusetts where he attended the Fenn School through grades 5 to 7. In 1944, his father married Florence Eaton Davis and their marriage lasted for thirty-four years. In 1946, Rowland moved with his father and stepmother to University City, Missouri, where he completed his secondary education. In 1987, his widowed father was married a third time to Nancy Gilson Davis, the daughter of an old friend, who saw to him until his death in 1992 at the age of 95.

After attending University City High School in St. Louis, Rowland went on to Harvard University for his undergraduate and graduate education to study molecular biology and microbial genetics. During his senior year at Harvard, he took a course on writing short stories in which one of his classmates was John Updike. Rowland notes that "Updike was very talented. He read his short stories and I read mine, both to mutual acclaim." At this time Rowland wanted to be a writer, but his interest in and further studies in biology pushed this ambition into the background. He received his Ph.D. from Harvard in 1958 and went on to an academic career that included serving as a National Science Foundation Fellow at the California Institute of Technology, a faculty appointment at the University of Michigan from 1960 to 1975, and a position as Professor of Molecular Biology and Biochemistry at the University of California, Irvine from 1975 until his retirement in 2004. In the course of his career he was appointed a Fellow of the American Academy of Microbiology and of the American Association for the Advancement of Science. His scientific interests eventually led him to write three books: *The Gist of Genetics*, co-authored with Stephen G. Weller in 1997; *Neurospora: Contributions of a Model Organism* in 2000; and *The Microbial Models of Molecular Biology* in 2003.

Although Rowland continued active professional and administrative service to the University of California, Irvine after his retirement, he now turned his attention to serious creative writing. He joined an online writing group called the International Writers Workshop whose support he found extremely valuable. The Workshop allowed him to share his stories with a group of other writers and receive quick feedback from many on his work, while providing the same service for them. At the same time his wife Margot Norris encouraged him to consider writing a mystery novel with her that would be set on the island of Crete, a site the couple had visited on two occasions and whose Istron Bay Resort seemed a perfect setting for the story. Collaboration on this work prompted Rowland and Margot to attend the Santa Barbara Writers Conference in 2007 in the hopes of securing the service of an agent. In May 2008 Rowland suffered a severe hemorrhagic stroke which left him in critical condition for two weeks and required four months of hospital care and extensive physical and occupational therapy before he was able to return home. Since their mystery novel *Murder at Astron Bay* was completed and ready for publication before the stroke, the couple proceeded to publish it with PublishAmerica in 2009. This work received numerous excellent reviews on Amazon. Rowland and Margot Davis subsequently published a second mystery novel, *Death in Laguna Beach,* which appeared in 2012. The present collection of short stories by Rowland Davis was produced during the decade from 2003 to 2013—both before his stroke and in the last two years since his stroke. His recent writing has been made possible thanks to Dragon, a program with speech recognition software that allows him to produce text on his computer without typing. *Lives and Loves: The Stories of Rowland Davis* covers a variety of human relationships in a variety of narrative styles. Rowland plans to continue writing short stories as long as Dragon enjoys listening to his voice.

TABLE OF CONTENTS

COUPLES

DR. MARSHALL IS DEAD

My name is Curtis Hoblin (my nickname used to be Hobgoblin, which I hated). I'm a philatelist—a fancy name for a stamp collector—and am retired and reasonably wealthy, so I have a great deal of time for my hobby. In addition, I travel a lot, again in connection with my hobby. I am also happily unmarried, which makes me free of all obligations of a matrimonial sort—such as sex (I get sufficient satisfaction from taking matters in my own hand) and cooking (except for myself). For breakfast, I make myself a soft-boiled egg with English muffins covered with honey. The trick to a soft-boiled egg is to remove the blunt end without messing up the shell as a whole. (I call this scalping.) It took me a while to learn this trick, but I managed, and I've gotten quite practiced at it. I buy my own clothes—one suit a year because I travel so much and I want to look my best at all times. I am sixty years old and took advantage of an early retirement program at my law firm.

I have been in the habit of sending misaddressed envelopes to exotic places with a note on the cover saying, "if undeliverable, please return to sender." I enclose a note saying something along the lines of: "I had heard you were deceased, but congratulations on the fact of your continued existence." My hope was to get an annoyed letter in return, with, of course, a treasured postage stamp from the foreign country on the envelope. This was not working at all well, so I developed another strategy. I decided to address my correspondence directly to the postmaster of the place of interest to me with a note on the envelope saying, "US stamps enclosed. Please open." In the letter enclosed, I would say, "I'm sending you these in hopes you can trade them for stamps of your own. I believe I have enclosed enough to make up for whatever I might owe you. I assume, without knowing whether you collect stamps or not, that you might be able to negotiate with other customers a similar trade." I would then sign it. 'C. Hoblin' with the subtitle 'philatelist' on the next line, and in parenthesis (stamp collector). This worked surprisingly well, given the stamps I brought in: about 5% replied, some with real interest, and many with thanks.

I had been looking on the Internet and found the name of Goa, a shoreline principality, later annexed by India after a brief dispute with Portugal. This was accomplished by Rajiv Ghandi in 1961. I had never been to Goa, which seemed attractive and exotic to me, but had planned to visit the place as soon as I had time. (I was in the market for Goan stamps, a rarity in my collection, if you must know.) The time never arose so I forgot all about it for the time being.

I was reminded of my suspended intention by a letter in the mail. It was a curious response to an old letter from someone I did not know. It was a real letter from a woman living in Goa. I had deliberately misaddressed a letter at one time to one Dr. Marshall. Because Goa is a small part of India, and because people there were widely known, owing to its small size, it had reached a woman having the same last name. Her letter began: "Dr. Marshall is dead." She wondered who might be seeking contact with him. I was shocked, shocked, having conjured up his very existence as well as his fictional demise purely out of my imagination. The woman went on to ask how I came to know him and filled me in on the circumstances of his death. "I am custodian of his estate since his death. As his widow, I need to ask if your relationship with my husband entails either money owed or credit in need of repayment. If you can prove your bona fides I will try to settle any financial issues with you. If necessary we can deal with matters in person, if you have occasion to visit Goa."

I thought of how to respond to this letter. My first instinct was simply to admit I was seeking stamps for my collection, which was innocent of stamps from Goa. My second instinct was to visit Dr. Marshall's widow in person, since it appeared—improbably again—that she would not object to meeting me. And I certainly felt wealthy enough to do so. My third instinct was to tear up the letter, and let the matter die (minus the stamp, of course) of its own accord. I thought hard about this dilemma for a short time. By that time, I discovered that I had thrown away the envelope with her return address. Luckily, I retrieved the envelope before the trash had been disposed of. I was so anxious to save the stamp that I had overlooked the lack of a return address in the body of the letter.

What to do? What to do? I asked myself this question many times in the next few weeks. The only option left to me was the second, I realized, after much thought. I could always address a letter to 'Mrs. Marshall' at the address on the corner of the envelope. So I sent a proper note to this lady, saying I would be glad to travel to meet her in order to discuss an important financial and personal matter. I did not admit that I was merely in quest of stamps for my collection, but I hinted that I was anxious to go to Goa as an adventure. I added, in haste, that I was terribly sorry for her loss.

I heard from her soon thereafter with a kind note saying she would be happy to make my acquaintance.

* * *

When I got to Goa (it has one international airport), I looked her up in the directory for foreigners, among them one in English. Goa is a prosperous small community in western India, which made me comfortable from the beginning. In fact, English was widely spoken, given the tourism which it had encouraged, even before it was annexed by India. I looked her up, and there she was, listed under the name of Sylvia Marshall, the only Marshall in the book. It was not improbable to find her listed in this way, and uniquely at that, since the name turned out to be uncommon in Goa.

I first thought of calling her but changed my mind and went to the address listed in the phonebook by cab. I knocked on the door of her house—assuming it was her house. When a woman opened the door, I said, "Mrs. Marshall, I presume," thinking of Stanley's famous quote as he met Livingston at the source of the Nile. She laughed, and I was surprised to find that she was affable and completely welcoming after I identified myself. Mrs. Marshall was about my age, but vigorous and attractive. She had white hair, and was obviously of English or American descent. "I have been waiting for you for some time," she said, as she reached out her hand to shake mine. "I'm so glad we meet." I was grateful for her command of

English rather than some foreign language. I immediately felt quite comfortable with her.

"Won't you step in?" she said, and led me to her well-furnished living room. It was easily the most beautiful room I had encountered in all my travels, with delightful drapes and luxuriant framed pictures on the walls, mainly of nautical subjects such as shells, jellyfish, sponges, and things that might attract tourists. Wide windows opened onto a beach. I could tell from the rich appointments that Dr. Marshall had been well-to-do. She was gracious, as I suspected she would be, and offered me a glass of wine as I sat down.

"So what is this pressing financial matter you have traveled half-way around the world to discuss with me?" she said, smiling, after we were settled with our goblets.

Now I was mortified. "I am here to offer an apology," I stammered. "I must confess that I was only seeking stamps from Goa all along. I had no idea that 'Dr. Marshall' was your husband, when I misaddressed a letter to a fictitious person hoping for a response with a stamp. But it accidentally found its way to you. This was a cruel mistake on my part, and I offer you my apologies."

She frowned. "Ah," she finally said, "and here I thought you had come to repay your ten thousand dollar debt to my husband."

"My what?" I said, shocked.

"Why, your payment for all the rare and valuable stamps he sent you in return. Did you not know he made copies of all the stamps he sent you, along with his invoices? Our attorney discovered them in his desk while processing our estate documents."

I was speechless. "Surely you know that I never received any such mailings from him?"

She looked at me steadily, though not coldly. "Would you like to see the copies?" she asked.

"Yes, yes," I blurted out. I was beside myself. It flashed through my mind that I had never mentioned stamps in my note to her. How could this be?

Seeing my stricken expression, she burst out laughing. She put a slender hand on my arm and said gently, "Now it is my turn to apologize. Forgive me." She suppressed another small laugh. "I could not resist turning the tables on you. There is no letter from Dr. Marshall, and he sent you no stamps. And now you need feel no guilt or remorse any longer."

I was not easily mollified. How could she play such a trick on me? She must have been reading my mind. After patting my arm again, she said gently: "I suppose you enjoy teasing people more than you enjoy being teased."

Then she rose from the sofa, and went into another room adjacent to where we were speaking. When she returned, she handed me a transparent envelope containing a variety of stamps. "These are all I have at the moment, but you are very welcome to them. I don't want you to feel you made this journey in vain."

I was angry no longer. I confessed that quite apart from stamps, I had always wanted to see Goa and asked if she might accept an invitation to accompany me in an exploration of its environs. This broke the ice, and we then got into conversation about Goa, its history, and many other things. It was enchanting to speak with her, and I felt more and more comfortable with her as the conversation went on. I forgot to look at my watch, and when I did I realized two hours had gone by. I jumped in surprise as I recognized what time I had spent with her.

As I rose to go, I fortunately remembered to invite her to dinner. It was Friday, and I felt I had to rest up at the hotel. I thought it would be best to invite her for Saturday. "Would you care to join me for dinner, at some place of your own choosing? Tomorrow? As you know, I am unfamiliar with Goa and need help finding my way around." She accepted immediately, and I then phoned for a taxi. (She kindly showed me how to use the phone.) I gave her the address of the hotel so she could meet me on Saturday. I left her as she politely closed the door behind me. I had been very courtly during our conversation.

* * *

She showed up promptly at seven o'clock at the hotel as planned. "I'm so happy to see you again, I wondered whether I had bored you by talking so much last time. It's a habit of mine, for which I hope you'll forgive me."

"Of course", she said. "Since the death of my husband, I have longed for conversation, and you are a good candidate for that."

"You are very kind, but I accept the compliment warmly."

"There are few candidates for civilized conversation, which I miss greatly. English is preserved chiefly for tourists, and my foreign languages are not so well developed."

"Since I am a recluse, I too need to keep my English polished," I told her. She raised her eyebrows a little at the word *recluse*, but didn't say anything.

She had chosen a lovely restaurant right on the beach. The tables were set on a patio outdoors, although we could also have taken a table right by the water, with our shoes in the sand. A red umbrella with batik designs stood over our table, and once the sun began to sink to the horizon, small twinkling lights came on right above us. The menu had many Indian options, but I ordered grilled chicken rather than something exotic. I was surprised that my partner ordered a bottle of Riesling. She explained that it would calm the spices of her Indian vegetable dish but still match up well with my chicken.

"What was your husband's profession?" I asked her, after our wine was served. "I assume it was a medical one, no?"

"No, he was a Ph.D. in marine biology and had taught for many years in Canada. He came here after his retirement, having decided we should take an exotic vacation. We stayed the remaining years of his life. He took up painting, of shells and jellyfish and things that would mean something to tourists. You have seen these in my house, if you looked around. He had remarkable success and made a good deal of money with what he called a hobby. I admire him most for that, finding a second career."

"What did you do in the meantime?" I asked.

"I just enjoyed myself," she said. "With the beach and the climate in Goa, we chose a shoreline house, and it couldn't have been nicer. Although since my husband's death I haven't been quite myself anymore."

"I'm so sorry," I said. "I wondered what you did without him."

"Window shopping, mainly, although I wish I could travel again. But traveling, even alone, is very expensive, and nothing compares to the prosperous Goa. So I have largely given up traveling, for now. By the way, you dress rather sharply."

I wondered what to say at this point. "I buy a new suit each year, because I travel so much. And this is the new suit I bought for the occasion of my trip to Goa. Thank you so much for commenting on it."

"You're entirely welcome," she said. "Do you mind if I call you Curt? Or Curtis?"

"Either one, I have few friends, and I answer to both And what may I call you?"

"Sylvia," she said.

She went on, "I wondered what you did besides stamp collecting? I assume you have other interests."

"I have given up my interest in law, and now spend my time traveling. Traveling gives me a great deal of pleasure, besides stamp collecting, which keeps me occupied in the off-hours. When, that is, I have exhausted the local stamp stores. It may sound dull, but it occupies my time beautifully."

"Where have you been in your travels?" she asked. It was an idle question, but I answered happily.

"All over the world. Europe, Africa, Asia, Canada, Great Britain, South America and of course I specialize in commemoratives from every US state in the union."

"'Of course'", she said in a mocking, but amusing tone. "Do you have any photographs taken in the course of your travels?"

"None at all, cameras are an encumbrance I'd rather not carry around on my travels."

We were slowly moving into personal territory, I felt. But I felt surprisingly comfortable with her, so I proceeded to continue. I asked her what she missed most since the loss of her husband, hoping she would answer with a neutral word or two.

Without hesitating, she answered, "His body." I was shocked at her candor and she looked puzzled by my expression. "When I say 'his body,' I of course mean his living presence, the evidence of his warm and living flesh near me." I was still shocked. "And interesting conversation," she added, now frowning at my surprise. "You're the first person I've met with a gift of gab, as they say in the US."

"Well, don't look at me," I said, hastily and defensively. "Am I really that interesting?" For the first time I felt real affection for her, even though she made me nervous and confused. But I thought I'd keep this to myself.

* * *

As she drove me home in her car, I was impressed by the prosperity of the district. I could not imagine a nicer place to vacation, even for the rest of one's life. I was surprised that she invited me on an outing followed by dinner, 'when I had the time'. I mentioned that I had all the time in the world, since Goa was becoming a major interest.

"What would you like to see?" she asked, when she picked me up on the next afternoon. I was surprised at the way she drove, rapidly, but expertly avoiding collisions. When I asked her about this when there was a pause and she replied, "I learned to drive in Canada and never lost my habits of caution." She looked at me and smiled and I wondered if she was teasing me again.

"Well," I said, "you seem very able." I tried to hide my anxiety by making it sound humorous.

We began our tour of Goa. The beaches were picturesque and the houses were well-built and attractive. There was a hint of the Portuguese past in the older buildings, which made it a historical and interesting treasure. It was a lovely, if somewhat nerve-wracking tour, given her driving. After an hour or two she asked if there was more I would like to see? "Stores? Stamps? Or would you like to go to my house and relax? It looks as though you need it." I did, after the swift driving around the island and the sleeplessness that still pursued me after the long trip to India.

"I would love to be at your place," I answered without thinking about it. "I would love to relax for a small moment or two." I wondered what I would do there, given my fatigue and my fading conversational skills.

* * *

I found myself waking up in confusion as to where I was. This was no hotel room. I remembered the conversation with Sylvia. I must have gone to sleep in the car. It was now past six o'clock! How did I get here? Did she drug me by putting something into the soda we bought at a stop on our tour? She had helped me out of the car, I now remembered. Then another blankness came over me. The second time I open my eyes, she was there, sitting calmly at the head of the divan on which I went to sleep.

"Would you care for an early supper," she said in a kind voice. "It's not an Indian custom to make it so early, much less a Portuguese one. I thought you might like it, since my husband and I brought the habit over from Canada."

I hesitated, still in confusion about where I was and what I was doing here. "How long have I slept? Have you been waiting for me to wake up?"

"No," she answered, "I've been preparing supper for you. I hope you'll be happy with it."

Did she drug me? Why would she? I had told her I would be happy to come to her home with her. I suddenly wanted to reach into my wallet to see if my credit cards were still there. All this time she was waiting patiently, as though she understood that I was only now waking from a sound sleep and needed time to orient myself once more.

"I must go and check on the rice," she finally said, and rose to return to the kitchen. "But I will return in a moment with a glass of wine for you."

Would she drug my wine? The rice in my supper? Why? She knew I was well-to-do and that I was a recluse. Perhaps she guessed that no one would miss me if I did not return from Goa. She was a reckless driver and could run over my body with her car and claim it was an accident. I wanted to bolt from this house, but would need transportation, and I could not remember how to use the telephone.

I heard her open the kitchen door and knew she would be back with the glass of wine. I was sweating.

"You are very kind," I said, as she handed me the glass of blood-red wine. I silently said what would have to pass as a prayer, and took a sip. "You must forgive me for staying well beyond my welcome. I can't thank you enough for the privilege of letting me go to sleep on your divan and for kindly offering me supper."

"Not a problem," she said, "I hope you will like my cooking."

* * *

Bliss, pure bliss, I said to myself of my life in Goa. It had lasted more than a decade since I met Sylvia. It never seemed to end, nor did I want it to. I have given up stamp collecting, and most of my fussy habits. After a decorous interval, I began sleeping with her, and learned how good sex could be even at our advanced ages. She was vigorous as usual, and complimented me on my prowess. I didn't believe her for a moment, but I thanked her for her kindness, in saying so.

We traveled all over India, which I enjoyed until we grew too old to manage anymore. We were in our mid-sixties when we returned to Goa for good. Once when we were making love, I heard Sylvia chuckle as we finished.

"What are you laughing about," I asked.

"Has anyone ever called you Hobgoblin? I just thought of this. It fits you to a T." It was the first time I smiled at my nickname.

DEWDROP

Under the single lamp by her bed, Randall read Donne and Shakespeare and Auden out loud, even after Lucetta had nodded off. The cadence of the lines comforted them even more than the words. Lucetta lay silent in morphine-muffled agony as unruly cells colonized and disabled one organ after another. She died in May, dignified and contained in the last spasms of her disease.

Randall began his new life with their black female lab, Goldie. He sat in the evening on the couch facing the garden, Lucetta's garden, waiting each day for night. Joy in love? Yes, but after that? Just pay the back taxes on the good years. What do you do with a pencil stub, a cigarette butt, or the rest of your life? Just let it rain. It's probably Goldie, he thought, that will keep my heart beating.

Over sixty-eight now, Randall kept to the routine, letting Goldie lead him on long walks. The elm-canopied streets led either to the campus or quickly out of town. Past orchards and antique stores, little farms and their pastures, cows looking curiously at him as he and the dog padded on the shoulder of the two-lane roads. Or into the park, a large old commons, complete with a World War I memorial obelisk, maintained as a tourist rest and community resource. It now lay at the edge of the newer business area, fenced with black wrought iron and crossed by small paths among the maples. Without Lucetta, it was Goldie's favorite place, where the dog met her kind with animated purpose and sniffs of greeting. The summer came, and even the glory of the blooming skies and high clouds over the whole Northeast failed to lift Randall's spirits. Only Goldie's bark or an acquaintance nodding in sympathy interrupted Randall's ruminations. He walked to campus with a slight stoop once a week for his rare correspondence. A perfect New England college town. He hardly recognized that August had arrived. At first he neglected the garden like he neglected his beard. In August he hired Lucetta's gardener back to mow the front lawn and tend the roses and perennials in back, a memorial now to—and of—his wife's devotion to beauty and to the earth.

* * *

Fall came and with it, Randall's obligation to teach his ever popular, freewheeling course in logic and the history of science.

"Can I see you for a bit?" Arnold, his department chairman, invited himself into Randall's office. He sat diffidently on the chair facing Randall across his desk. Arnold, once a quarterback, still had some red in his hair and faded freckles across his pale face. On the wall behind Randall hung an autographed photo of Paul Feyerabend. Next to it dangled a stuffed jester with a crown and Randall's faculty portrait for a face. A gift from his students two years ago, celebrating Randall's sixty-fifth birthday and forty years of good-natured, iconoclastic teaching. Arnold looked at these artifacts and forced a smile as he leaned forward in his chair, feeling his stubble. "I wondered whether we could do anything for you."

"How do you mean?" Randall set last year's lecture notes aside on the computer keyboard. He could guess what was coming. Arnold was pretty shy these days, and dressed more like he had just come from his carpentry shop than from the chairman's office. His broad face had hollowed, and the heartiness of the smile under his bushy brows was gone. Randall felt a kinship with shaggy Arnie, who had been kicked out of his own house in the summer.

"A semester off or something?" A September rain fell gently outside the window from a gray sky. The quadrangle outside was empty but for a student couple huddled under a single umbrella, hurrying with arms around each other to stay close, to stay dry.

Randall looked back at his old friend. "Won't make much difference. Teaching keeps me busy."

"It isn't making your students busy, from what I hear."

"They shouldn't complain. More time for sex. It's only the third week. I'm fine."

"C'mon, Randy. I know you're down, but I have to keep this place going. I have enough trouble with Deb and Lakshmi."

"I know. Sorry. But do you want me out of here? I could retire today if you want."

"I didn't say that. I know it must be hard to be your clever old self, but it may come back if you have some time off. Have you got anything distracting going, writing, a wish for travel?"

"Yeah. Solitaire, coffee, crosswords. I'm teaching Goldie German." He felt a bit of anger glowing like embers in the back of a cave.

"Well, I'd like to help, so let me know how I can. We've been together a long time. Us oldsters need a bit of dusting off once in a while." Arnold rose and leaned awkwardly over the desk, touching Randall on the shoulder. "Okay? And let's get together for a drink or lunch sometime soon."

"Okay. Thanks. I'll stay out of trouble." Randall gathered his notes, went to the lecture hall and began an extemporaneous lecture on free will, God's biggest mistake outside of pangolins and mosquitoes. Randall's reputation for wittily challenging philosophical heroes had attracted many students and auditors in his day. The students now looked covertly at each other, then sat back and looked at the ceiling lights as Randall went on with his lecture, all dead history and abstraction. Not good for the third week of class. Randall stopped fifteen minutes short of the hour. He waited for the students to leave before him, shuffling his superfluous papers. He straightened up and strode out behind them. Let's get the old act together. It's always been an act. It's always worked until now. Poor sods.

* * *

The phone rang.

"Hi Randy."

"Hi Deb." It was a late Wednesday evening in early October. He lay stretched on the couch and nestled the phone to his ear by his shoulder. Goldie sniffed at the remains of Randall's meal on the coffee table and jumped onto the couch. Randall bent his knees to make room for her.

"How're you doing, Randy? Don't worry, your casserole days are over."

"I'm relieved. My freezer is still full."

"You should eat more."

"I don't hunger for anything. I'm eating. I'm fine." He reached for his glass. The ice had melted, and he was glad Deb wouldn't hear it clinking on the phone.

"Do you want some company?"

"Only if you want some yourself." At least I can be nice, he thought. Other people's miseries are tastier than mine, and might offer company in the dark. Deb had her own problems since Arnold moved out. "Come over if you like."

She appeared in twenty minutes, walking from her place up the street. Goldie barked even before the doorbell rang. A brief hug. He was glad he'd cleared off his supper remains before she arrived, knowing that she would comment on how he'd let himself go. She was a tidy lady, but plain enough to escape notice at a party. Dyed straight brown hair, thick at the waist, wearing a plum dress better suited to a thinner woman. Doughy face, no eyebrows. Oddly, Arnie's departure had made her more outgoing.

"Drink?"

"I guess. Scotch? On ice?" Her small black eyes widened, looking like marbles in putty.

"No problem. Have a seat." She sat beside his place on the couch facing the garden as he went to fetch her drink. He returned, taking a seat in an uncomfortable wooden chair facing her. The garden door was open in spite of the October chill, and he heard two cats yowling, the only traffic this late in the small town. He put on a clinical smile and leaned forward. "So what's happening?"

She frowned. "I was about to ask you, Randy."

"I asked first. Are things settling down with you guys?" Arnold had taken up with the new hire, Lakshmi Kupur, a slender Indian linguist with dark, velvet skin and bottomless eyes. Deb had made it a public affair with irreversible marital damage. Both Deb and Arnold had told him their versions. He thought a good deal less of both of them now, but still couldn't help feeling sympathetic, at least to Arnold. His poor old friends floundered about like fresh-caught trout in the bottom of a rowboat.

"Arnie's fine, I expect, just fine." She frowned again. "She could have anyone she wanted. But why Arnie? He's old. Good riddance. I wish they'd just get out of town. Move to some place like Regina, Uppsala, Baffinland. Or India for all I care." Deb paused to sip her scotch. "I'm no beauty, Randy, and never was, but after that long, you'd think…" Handkerchief. "I mean, what can I do? Arnie may have had a wandering eye now and again, but he never strayed like this. At least Lucy didn't leave you."

"Deb, let it go. You booted him, and you'll make adjustments like I did. Just don't bring Lucetta into it."

"Sorry. I was here to see how you were." She dabbed the corner of both eyes. She took another swig from her drink, plainly not her first that night. "I shouldn't have come over. I should go." Yes, Randall thought, you should go before I have to listen to your angry, mournful story again. With your righteous streak that brooks no argument, accepts no comfort, and turns scotch straight into salty, bitter, unforgiving tears. If I were Arnie…

Randall brought this silent rant to a close as he showed her out. She held his hand for just a moment, but pleaded with her eyes to cuddle with him forever. Her plainness evoked by contrast Lucetta's smiling eyes, handsome white hair, lovely cheeks, confident jaw. He wondered how Deb would ever get on alone. In her cups last winter, she'd come onto him. Her breath stank, and he took her by the shoulders and turned her sideways with a brotherly hug. Easy, Deb, he'd said. She had left and they went on, never speaking of it again.

Deb turned on the path to the sidewalk. "If you see Arnie, let him know he can have the cat. She misses him."

"Like I told you, Deb, no messenger service. Write him. Sorry."

"I know. Sorry. Call sometime." She went into the dark and up the street. He wondered how he himself would ever get on alone. But there must be worse fates.

* * *

"Randy."

"Hi Arnie. What's up?"

"Thought you might like to do lunch. You busy?"

"Fine."

Davey's had a booth open, and they ordered right away. A beer and a dog for both.

"How's everything?" Randall had learned to ask first.
Arnie sat opposite, his face showing deeper creases. He leaned forward, his broad shoulders stretching his threadbare Harris tweed. "I was about to ask you. You seem to be getting some of your old bounce back."

"It's an act."

"Class going well?"

"Better. But those empty minds are about as nimble as starfish. First week in the fall was like talking to a bunch of black holes. For them, the mind-body problem is about minding each others' bodies. Animals all. How about you?"

"Fine." Arnold began to twist his napkin. "Randy, I wondered whether you'd seen Debbie?"

"A week ago. She's okay, but that's all I can say."

"No, I mean, is she really getting on okay?"

"I said she's okay. I'm not the Western Union. You may want to get in touch with her."

"Can't. She's pretty hostile. Can't blame her. Makes me feel like a fucking worm."

"Just to change the subject, how's Lakshmi? Things working out?" Perverse question, but relevant, to say the least.

"Not really. I'd just as soon let it go for now."

"So what's the problem?" A promising conversation shouldn't end so quickly, Randall mused. Here's Arnie, confiding in me more since Lucetta died, talking to me like I was a font of insight and advice. But it's fine, his troubles are toys for reflection, irony ore. At least he knows I'm honest, and at least I'm not cruel to his face.

"I'm adjusting," Arnold said.

Randall looked back from the window. He felt for a moment he'd been in outer space, floating weightlessly away from the mother ship. "Great," he said, "probably good to take it in steps, not too fast. She's young and new here, and she's got a job to do."

"Fact is…" The waiter interrupted, setting the franks and beers down before them.

"What?"

"Nothing."

"Tell me." Randall took a bite.

"Fact is, she thinks I'm too old for this, and she has too much to lose if things get more complicated at work. She wants out."

"Well. I guess I'm sorry. But as a friend, I say you should take her seriously. In case you hadn't noticed, you're in an exposed position too. But it's none of my business."

"Randy, bear with me. I need advice. What do you hear in the halls?"

"Not a lot. People know we're old friends and don't say much to me."

"Randy, I know it's stupid what I got myself into. The summer made it feel safe, you know, 'just this once' kind of thing. I was a dotty old fart for thinking it could continue. Now she tells me she thought my approach was sort of a hospitality program for new faculty. Believe it or not, that's what she said."

"Well, at least she has a sense of humor. I'd say you'd better get out while the getting's good. I know how you feel, but you could wind up out of here. You may have burned bridges with Deb, but you could really screw up your short future. Royally. And hers. I mean Lakshmi's."

"How can I argue?" He looked at his plate, at his uneaten frank. By now shreds of napkin had littered the area around it. "Thanks for listening, it's a big help. I knew all this to begin with, but Deb sort of marooned me. I don't even have a right to feel sorry for myself. To tell you the truth, I'm not hungry. Let's go."

Yes, there *were* worse fates. Just being the prim Deb or even the dutiful Arnie of old was bad enough, but they should have just stayed under their rock, squirming in the dark.

* * *

"Dr. Carson?"

"Hello. Who is this?" He got few calls at home now.

"It's Lakshmi Kupur, your new colleague. I wonder if I could talk to you."

He should have picked up on the Oxford Indian accent. Randall felt the hair on the back of his neck rise. Sunday, almost a week after talking to Arnie, no less. "What about?"

"It's personal, as you can imagine. Are you free sometime this week? Soon?" Her voice was strong, claiming respect. He pictured her at the last faculty meeting, clad in a white sweater and black slacks. She had a habit of running her black hair through her fingers, curling it oddly around her chin, over and over. Her black eyes looked out from under her brow as she sat silent and otherwise motionless for the whole meeting. Quiet as she was, the twelve faculty members, men and women, felt her presence. And Arnie, with his eyes darting about, plainly had trouble running the meeting.

"I'm not sure I can help you much, if it's what I think it is."

"Arnold said he'd had a word with you. He said you might offer me some advice, objective advice. I'm sad and frightened, as much for Arnold as for myself. You know our situation, and I can scarcely talk to anyone else. It took me more than a few sleepless nights to call you."

"I'm an old horse, Lakshmi, going to pasture soon. I've had my own problems, as you probably know. How would I be able to help?" Randall realized that he was almost whispering, even in the privacy of his home. The dew of his breath had condensed on the mouth of the receiver.

"Listening would be a start. I'm sure you've accumulated some wisdom, some philosophical wisdom, over the years. I would profit from a few long moments."

"Okay. I can listen." Damned right, Randall thought. A faculty soap opera is all a widowed philosopher needs to confirm the folly of academic life. Like Arnie coming back from the undead while he's still strong enough to do something really stupid.

She came by his house in her Celica late the next afternoon, just after he had decided what to wear. A little warm for the tweed, but the blazer would do. He had trimmed his beard because it was Monday and the barber was closed. The back seat of her car was filled with file boxes. She drove without much conversation to the Delhi, a new, modest, out-of-town Indian restaurant on Route 9. It stood near some isolated older houses by a new hairdresser's shop and a Chevron station with a minimart. An open field lay across the road beyond a gray, cross-timbered fence. Lakshmi already knew the restaurant's waiters and the owner. A small place with a curtain of beaded strings in an arch as an entry from the foyer. White walls, white tablecloths, and the slow, soft plang of sitar music.

After they were seated at a back table, Lakshmi leaned forward on the tablecloth, self-possessed as ever. "I'm sorry if this is embarrassing for you. It certainly is to me, so don't feel undone by the occasion." She smiled, her narrow lips parting to reveal even teeth, white as the walls, contrasting magnificently with her dusty Tamil skin.

"I can't be undone at my age." This woman scares me.

"May I call you Randall?"

"Of course."

"Well, as you know, I'm in trouble, trouble I could easily have avoided. I've lived in America now for ten years. It was a liberated life in San Francisco after I came here, and I did some stupid adolescent things there, things I could never do in India and would never do again." She took a deep breath. "At least I became a free woman, but one can make rather bad uses of freedom even at the age of thirty-two. Especially in a small college town where privacy is at a premium." Lakshmi seemed out of words despite her steady look. She laced her fingers together, her elbows on the table. Surprisingly delicate arms for such an assured, articulate woman.

"I'm listening. I'm not sure where you're headed. Will you have something to drink?" The waiter had come to the table.

"Oh, Krish, hello. Yes."

They looked at their menus and ordered wines and two curries with rice to share. The two looked beyond each other for a few moments after the waiter left, awkwardly feeling their silverware.

Randall broke the silence. "So how do you see your situation?"

"It depends more than a little on how you and your colleagues see my situation."

"I can't tell you much. I don't see enough of them. Where do you two stand now?"

"A bit apart, as you know. Arnold and I were both lonely when I got here in June. He helped me set up in my flat. It was so good of him, the chair, to do that."

"We're a hospitable department. Family, in a way."

"Well, he made a sweet pass at me and I thanked him in all too sincere a way. But I needed that. He needed it more, it seems, but I thought it would not lead to anything, at least by the time the fall semester started. You know the rest. Especially after Deborah put it about to the faculty, which drove him to me all the more. I've had men fall for me, but Arnold? At his age, he should have known how to keep it light and brief. He had too much to lose, and now I do too."

"So?"

"I won't burden you with the 'relationship,' as one politely puts it, except that Deborah has made her house a point of no return for Arnold. The question for me, in a nutshell, is whether I should try to leave the college. I don't feel I'm wholly to blame, but everyone else doubtless thinks so. It would minimize damage all around. Unhappily, I have nowhere to go."

"I'd hate to see you leave, Lakshmi. We bid pretty high for you and everyone was thrilled that you came. Actually, this may all blow over." Keep it easy, he thought, I'm just here to listen to this smart, gorgeous, mortal fool. For all I know, she might take up with other faculty members and show how liberated she really was. Good for the department's morale.

Randall's sadness had stirred up darker sediments of his critical insight. In May, just before Lucetta died, Randall remembered an aimless November walk he had taken in the night streets of Cambridge forty-five years before. Dry leaves blew about him as he struggled with his emptiness, getting a grip on himself. He looked to his right and saw his dim reflection in a darkened store window, almost a silhouette with a street light behind him. He faced his image and wondered, (as undergraduates do, he would say later), whether that was the real Randall Carson. As he looked, a light came on in the store and his reflection vanished.

"Randall?"

"What? I'm sorry. I had a moment there. Go on."

"I was saying one of the jobs I turned down last spring is still open. But it would be hard, to say the least, to explain why I might be reapplying."

"You're nothing if not realistic. It's October, and you can hardly leave without serious inconvenience all around. And they're not hiring in the fall anyway, I suspect."

"I'm resigned to that. I can keep a low profile and stick to my book and teaching. I've already made some friends in the Indian community here." She waved vaguely at the room around her. "I've lived long enough to know how to be content alone if need be."

That makes one of us, Randall thought. "You're right. As I often say, some problems die of neglect. You'd just have to wait it out. I wish I could help in the meantime, but I don't see how."

"Maybe you could be more help with Arnold. We haven't been together for the last six weeks, and I don't want to be. It's hard to talk on the phone. He used to call a good deal more than I like. I've gotten caller ID. If you have a chance, tell him I'm sympathetic, but it's over and I wish him well. And that he's not the only one with a problem."

"I'm not a go-between, Lakshmi, but I will if the moment's right."

"That's more than I can ask. Here's Krish with the food." The waiter set the curried lamb and chicken and rice down between them. "I've imposed terribly on you, Randall, and I'm sorry. But thanks so much for listening. Especially in your situation. I hope things are going better for you these days." Her shoulders relaxed, and she smiled gently, beautifully. "Why don't you tell me about your work?" She kept smiling, enough to melt the Arctic.

"I'm a critic, Lakshmi, not really a scholar. I was planning to take on some of the young theorists. But they already did my work for me—they're parodies of themselves." He warmed to her, smiling more broadly than he had in months. "I pity them, but I keep that to myself."

His spirit was back. What a difference good company makes!

* * *

They finished the curry, almost oblivious to its taste, engrossed as they were in Randall's run-down of the ins and outs of their eclectic Cultural Studies department. He shared some of the *bon mots* he used to twit his colleagues. He'd named a faculty member, a student of semiotics, an Eco-freak and sometimes mused that Marxism was the 'opiate of the professoriate.'

"Very good," Lakshmi broke in, smiling under her dark brow. "Even Marx would have enjoyed that. You know, some Marxists display surprising intelligence, but ideology isn't my style."

After more of this and another round of wine, Randall said, "Tell me what you are up to, then, Lakshmi. I read your file, but couldn't make your job seminar last spring."

Lakshmi paused to collect her thoughts. "Well, my book is on several Indian languages, of which there are more than a few, as you must know. I'm highlighting a community, the Purudan, whose sexes are so segregated, and at such an early age, that the women actually use a separate dialect, an old one, among themselves. The men and boys grow up speaking a more modern version. The females can actually practice a secret feminism, with a much greater solidarity than you see in other sects. I was really quite lucky to be able to do my field work before they were exposed much to newer ways."

"That sounds a bit scary, at least to a male. I'm not sure I could feel secure."

"People say that, and it may be true. I was unable to interview the men satisfactorily, so that's a remaining problem. The situation reminded me of twin-talk, a little language of their own. But enough. Let me settle up. It's warm and light enough perhaps to have a walk. It's lovely out here, so different from the city or where I grew up in India. Krish?"

Randall did not dispute her offer to pay. She stood up in a single fluid motion as she wrapped her light white shawl about her shoulders. They went out into the October dusk and crossed the road from the parking lot.

"I understand from Arnold that you've had a very difficult time in the last year, Randall. He's quite concerned for you." Walking on the dirt shoulder of the road had made Randall feel relaxed, but her remark took him by surprise.

"I know. I'm getting over it. We all have to at times like these."

"I'm sorry if I'm intrusive. Arnold talked about it when we were together, and even thought I might be able to help. You've been so good to me today that I felt I should ask. Maybe just so you can talk. You are alone, aren't you?"

Jesus, where is this going? Randall once again felt the hairs on his nape rise, a dangerous little thrill. "Yep," he said. "Except for Goldie." She looked at him. "My dog. Me and Lucetta's." The joy he felt in the restaurant had evaporated. His breath was short.

"I'm so sorry. She must have been the light of your life. Lucetta. It's a rather old-fashioned name, isn't it?"

"Yep. After her great aunt." This Lakshmi does get to the point. Randall understood Arnie better now. Something is happening to me after these months. He was glad it was getting dark.

Lakshmi remained silent for a time. "Where did you grow up, Randall?"

"Utica. Small town outside of Utica. My father had an antique shop, and he and my mother were starved for culture out there. They grew up in Boston. Read everything. I caught it from them."

"Sounds like a good start. Are they still with us?"

"Let's turn around. I think it's going to be dark soon. No, my parents are gone. Mother died when I was twelve. Dad drifted off after that, but only lived to be fifty-five. He never got over it." They turned back along the fence.

"How very sad. So you saw real unhappiness early on. It must have been a formative moment, losing your mother then. May I ask how she died?"

"Suicide. The usual sleeping pills." Randall had never volunteered this, even to Arnold.

"Oh, I'm so sorry. Forgive me for asking." Lakshmi raised her hand and briefly touched Randall's shoulder. "I'm sorry for being so outspoken. Will you forgive me?"

"Nothing to forgive. It was good of you to ask. I just haven't dealt with it for some time." Randall strangled on the words. "I think we should get back to town."

"Of course. I'm so sorry. This was so nice, and I'm afraid I've offended you. I should never have waded into your life like that."

They reached the place to cross back to the parking lot.

"Please don't worry, Lakshmi."

They got into the car and Lakshmi, without turning to him said, "Randall, I hope we can be friends. I feel immensely better. Can I change the subject? Why don't you tell me how you came to be so damned well educated." She turned and smiled as she drove onto the road and turned on the headlights.

The dam was about to give. "Harvard. After Harvard, you can fake anything." With his right hand, he brushed a tear from his eye.

"You're a modest man, Randall. And a wise one. Enough to find comfort, even happiness. Just let it happen."

They rode in silence back to Randall's place. There was just too little, too much to say. As he prepared to leave the car, he and Lakshmi turned to one another. She moved slowly toward him and kissed him gently on the mouth. She whispered. "Good night. And thank you so much."

Randall went quickly into his house, with a little wave to the still motionless car as he went in the door. The car moved off as he turned on his lights and went into the living room area. Goldie, leaving a warm spot on the couch facing the garden, came to him. Randall took his seat in his familiar place on the couch, and wept and wept and wept for the first time since Lucetta died. Let it rain. Let it pour.

Goldie jumped up and licked the salty cheeks of her master, her only friend.

* * *

Evolution, Randall thought, gave us wolves, and from them humans had made dogs, shaping their behavior with breeding and training. Goldie ferreted out lizards and mice in the garden, barked at pets and people beyond the back fence, and followed Randall dutifully about the house. Randall walked her in the park every day, a job Lucetta had done religiously since they acquired her as a pup. Goldie had interest, purpose, and some months ago the comfort of Lucetta's indulgence. What did Goldie know? Nothing, really. Expectations built of experience, of habit. Walks, meals, homecomings. A happy, meaningless life, like those of most of Randall's colleagues. A life Goldie resumed with her remaining master within a month after Lucetta had gone, grief now behind her. We humans too have evolved, he thought, blindly making up purposes and goals out of thin air, buoyed by love and ego. The ill-trained dogs of muddled gods.

* * *

At Christmas, Randall reflected on Lucetta's early unhesitating smile, her unwillingness to question life, her resolute love that closed the door on Randall's starless world. "It's what you think, Randy, that's what's meaningless. Enjoy what you do best. Help your poor colleagues, all of us, to think. It's your God-given talent, and I never want to be without you." He had become a holy fool, spreading cheerful cleanliness to the thoughts of others, reaping the ephemeral joys of being their witty, intellectual janitor. Without Lucetta, Randall had lived on in a darker, airless world, where he felt he had become dislikable, helpless to rekindle the bright kindness that had made him so admired.

And then in a single evening, Lakshmi's quiet, radiant smile had brought his anger to an end. The tears, reserved for more than a year, tears reserved since he was twelve, spilled from him as he recalled how she told him to let it happen, as she kissed him in thanks for his help, as his own heart burst with howling relief and let him revert to the winning, clever mortal Lucetta had made of him.

* * *

Even a year later, he still asked himself how Lakshmi could smile that way, with confidence and decency even at the peak of her difficulties. Her smile alone had rekindled some of the stars that had vanished when Lucetta died. During the year after their evening, he helped Lakshmi with her work, but he never saw her outside the college again. A curious intimacy surrounded them, undisturbed by the two men in her life. The first was Krishna from the family who owned the Delhi Restaurant. The second was a former lover from her San Francisco days. The intimacy with Randall was one of heart and mind, one to be consummated only by joint intellectual effort, with her in the lead. That was something that even Lucetta could not give him, and Randall grew into his role, giving coherence and structure to her efforts. He toyed again with the limits of wordy arguments, flaws of logic, and the vacancy of human souls around him. He came to admire joy without purpose, beauty without truth, even if he remained skeptical of both.

He talked more now with Arnold when he came over, or at Arnold's apartment, or at Davey's, convincing him that there was life after divorce, as there was for Randall now. He would find it. Just let it happen. He suggested that both of them retire in June in a joint ceremony to relieve the department of its past. Later in the summer, Randall helped Arnold clear his old house, now Deb's, of his tools and move them to a place in town he had rented so Arnold could indulge his ambition to be a full-time cabinet maker.

With her divorce, Deb no longer drank much. Her hair was curled, and a make-over brought out the beauty of her bright eyes. "Randy," she said once after a long talk, "I was always intimidated by you and Lucy, your marriage. Arnie and I just felt we were failures. Not just together, but even alone. You helped so much in the last few months for me to see that Lucy could renew herself every day. My friend Jonathan is a little like you, and I think that's why we got together. I have to thank both you and Lucy. Inspiring. I hope you find someone for yourself. I even hope Arnie finds someone. We've talked a few times, but I know he's still a little lost."

Early on a sunny morning in August, Randall followed Goldie into the garden in the sun. The dog barked twice to admonish a passer-by far away. Randall's heart skipped a beat, and then another. He fell to his knees next to the flower bed. He looked at one of Lucetta's prime red rose bushes close to him. A drop of dew lay on the largest petal of yesterday's blossom. Rounded like a paperweight, the dewdrop drank in the morning sun, condensing the world and Randall into a tiny memory, sharp as art glass, soon to disappear. He died, envious of the busy, barking dog, who would begin to mourn her second loss that very night.

SWEET CAROLINE

I met Caroline when we were on our knees in a bookstore looking for art books. They were large, and we found ourselves seeking the same kind of book. Her hair and eyes attracted me immediately upon seeing her. Our eyes met, and as I remembered it, I was riveted. She cropped her dark hair closely—it was almost black, as were her eyes—violet almost like Liz Taylor's—and she had a habit of batting her eyelashes while she talked. Her lips were full, and she had no difficulty smiling a lot. Her smile carried a tinge of irony, suggesting a strong personality, which I discovered later was not far off the mark.

She was looking for Monet illustrations, and I was looking for a book written by Salvador Dali. Still kneeling, we struck up a brief conversation, and I realized in the course of it that I wouldn't find the Dali autobiography there. But I then found some things I *did* want. I accompanied her to the cashier, and we conversed, while we were waiting in line. She seemed unaccompanied, and on a whim I invited her for coffee as we made our purchases. I introduced myself as Brendon McGill, and she gave her name as Caroline Jennings.

I discovered that she was unmarried, and in fact, had no boyfriend, having moved into town very recently. We were about the same age (she was twenty-six; I was twenty-five) and the conversation was quite easy. So easy, in fact, that I was tempted to ask her out for dinner that night. I did so on a whim and she accepted. At the time, I was finishing a doctoral thesis in history, and she was about to begin doctoral studies in biology.

Happily the small restaurant where we met had a table for two available in a quiet corner.

"So," I opened up, "I myself am a historian, you'll be happy to know, if you're interested. If you're not, I won't go on boring you. Are you interested in history? I don't suppose you are, being a biologist."

"I never took a history course in my life," she answered strongly but with a smile, suggesting a sense of humor.

Our mutual interest in art—a hobby for both of us—had brought us fortuitously together, so we abandoned history and biology and talked about art. She was attracted to the Impressionists, while I was attracted to Surrealism of the Dali-esque sort. I'll never forget the moment in the Bunuel movie, *Un Chien Andalou*, where—in a moonlit scene—an eyeball is sliced with a straight razor from corner to corner of the eye, or where Dali himself had ants coming out of his armpit. I was about to mention this but decided not to, out of fear that she would think me strange. I had taken a few courses in the history of art, and that is where I got my enthusiasm for the subject. As we spoke it was clear that our tastes differed substantially, but I was more familiar with her interests than she with mine. I had little taste at the time for Impressionist art, but was glad I could respond to her commentary. We talked until—to our surprise—we were asked to leave because the restaurant was closing.

* * *

The subject of my doctoral thesis was the French Revolution inspired by the film about the assassination of Marat by Charlotte Corday, often abbreviated as *Marat/Sade* but with the full title of *'The Persecution and Assassination of Jean-Paul Marat as Performed by the Inmates of the Asylum of Charenton Under the Direction of the Marquis de Sade'*. It was a surrealist movie, to my mind, and therefore suited my tastes beautifully. However, I soon found the research into Jean-Paul Marat's writings and newspaper publication tedious, and as a result toiled through the dissertation without much enthusiasm in spite of the support of my doctoral advisor. This led to a bit of soul-searching. It was then that I considered going into art professionally, not as a critic but as a painter. I wasn't anywhere near the draftsman that Dali was; nor did I have the imagination to produce distorted figures and limp clocks. But I made good sketches and wanted to advance my skills. I had been offered a job teaching history at a local community college in New Haven, so I hoped I was secure for a few years after finishing the dissertation. And my parents might support me if and when I ran out of money. They knew I was planning to paint in my free time, summers mainly, and they liked my artistic bent.

This left me with the question of what to do about Caroline, with whom I had fallen deeply and irreversibly in love. I was timid by nature, and I hadn't yet got the gumption to mention the word love to her. I was slowly becoming aware that she was dressing better and better. She was slender, and now wore slinky black pants with a green top modeled on a print by

Monet. She also gained more confidence, so much so that she could initiate conversations very easily, which compensated for my shyness.

"I've noticed that your clothes are improving over time," I said tentatively, "and I like them very much. Your Monet prints are great, and your new pants are very sexy."

"I thought you'd never notice," she replied, looking at me with some surprise. "I figured you were indifferent to such things."

"Me? You know I have an interest in art, or hadn't you noticed? I'm even beginning to like Monet and not only because of your wardrobe. Impressionism is gaining an attraction with me."

"I thought you were obsessed with Dali and Dali alone," she said. "I even thought of dressing as a surrealistic monster, with drawers coming out of my chest, to get your attention"

"Perish the thought!" I shook my head. "No, I've developed an affinity for Impressionism lately, but mainly for the Van Gogh sort."

"Wonderful! I thought you'd come around eventually." She smiled. "I think you're a very funny person and a good companion."

I felt I had to prove her last point, so I said, "Tell me if you've heard this one: as women dress in shorter and shorter skirts, I breathe in shorter and shorter pants." We both laughed, and I felt really good as I walked her to her rooming house.

"You are a *very* funny man," Caroline said when we reached her door. "You may kiss me if you like." I did so, brushing her cheek with my lips, but she did not invite me in. "Too many other girls there," she said

* * *

"Caroline, do you have something to tell me? You looked troubled."

"As a matter of fact, I do," she answered hastily, "I wondered whether I could share your apartment." This was stated boldly, as if it were in the front of her mind. I was taken aback, because she had never asked this before, and was shocked at her bringing this up so quickly after my recent chaste kiss. It turned out that her parents had suffered some financial difficulties. She could apply for financial aid to help with her graduate studies, but her parents could no longer pay for her rent even in her rooming house, given the expensive environs of New Haven where we both lived.

What would this mean for me? I asked myself. I thought it would be a nice arrangement, if my landlord could countenance another tenant in the apartment without charging more. Luckily, he was amenable to the idea, after talking with Caroline.

But what to do about sleeping arrangements? Much as I yearned for us to sleep together, I dared not hope that this was part of the deal. Three months after we met, I was still reluctant to ask her about this or to make any explicit moves of a sexual nature. She was just too nice to endanger our relationship that way. So I was stunned when she broached the topic in her usual straightforward way.

I was helping her clear out her apartment when she said, "We're on a new footing now." I was looking at all her Matisse prints and stopped packing them to hear what she meant. She suggested we share my bed and said she looked forward to having sex with me. I couldn't believe my ears.

"I have a strong attraction to you, and I've looked forward to this moment from the day I met you," Caroline said.

I was dumbfounded. "Same here," I said. "The same is true of me. When we met in the bookstore, I couldn't take my eyes off you."

"Why didn't you give me a hint as to your feelings about me? It would have been easy as sin (which it would've been) for you to do so." She gave me a saucy smile.

"Because I didn't want to endanger our relationship," I answered, "You know, women are different than men when it comes to this sort of thing. I'm sorry I didn't consider that you might be completely different from the few other women I've met."

After we unpacked Caroline's things in my apartment, I blurted out, "I'm so glad that our relationship has endured to this point." I took a deep breath. "And perhaps forever." This was the first time I had said anything about love, or a permanent relationship. We were in the bedroom, and upon hearing this, Caroline tumbled into my double bed, and gestured for me to follow.

Her slender legs were even more attractive than when she was dressed. Her breasts were small and quite well formed. Her hair had grown out longer and fuller, which made her look even more stunning than when I first met her in the bookstore. And what she could do with her full lips was quite remarkable. At first, it was a matter of kissing me all over. Then she sucked my big toe, a highly erotic gesture, if you've ever experienced it. Then she boldly inserted her tongue into my mouth, exercising it for a long time. I was underneath her, and she embraced me with her legs until I was within her. I came almost immediately, but stayed hard for a long minute with a pleasure I had not experienced with any of the brief encounters I had had before. She admitted that she too had come, but I had not noticed in the throes of my own pleasure. I felt that I had found true love at last.

"Did you like that?" She asked sweetly. "I thought you might come twice."

"I almost did!" I replied emphatically. "I hoped it would never end. I haven't said this before, but I love you more than you can imagine."

She smiled with a glow. "I've stayed on the Pill, just waiting for you to make the first move," she said. "I thought you'd never ask!"

"I was afraid to do so," I replied shyly. "But now that I've done it, I feel highly rewarded. And I'm glad you're on the Pill. It's a great relief to me to know this. I worried about that when we started but I was afraid to ask. And I didn't have time to ask you whether I should wear a condom." Caroline was clearly more experienced in sexual matters that I was. I was afraid to ask about her sexual history, so I let it go for the time being. Perhaps I never would ask, and as time passed, I never did.

* * *

I finished my dissertation in June, but without fanfare. My parents were away at the time of the commencement, so Caroline attended alone. Upon reflection after the ceremony, I felt I wanted to take a vacation with sweet Caroline in France, if she would agree. I had begun to call her *sweet* Caroline from the time we made love. I was fluent in French, owing to my year's visit to France in connection with my doctoral thesis, and hoped that Caroline would be free to go with me. (I would not have gone without her.) Since we were even more in love than we were the first night we had intercourse, I hoped upon hope that she could arrange an absence from her studies in biology during this summer after her first year. I had planned to paint if she were willing to go to France in the summer.

"I would be happy to take a summer leave of absence," she said. "I am frankly bored studying the sex life of morels. After living with you for a year, they seemed terribly unexciting in contrast." She had not lost her characteristic touch of irony. "I'm thinking of shifting my focus to crabs and other crustaceans and I can do that in France as well as in any other place."

She had not previously mentioned her dissatisfaction with her project, and I wondered if it was wise for her to make a decision at this time.

"You're right," she agreed. "I need time to think about this choice, and a vacation would give me the space to do that. I would enjoy a trip to France very much indeed. It'll also give me a chance to brush up on my French. I haven't had much practice with it since my days in boarding school."

"Fine!" I said, "I'll get airplane tickets and make other reservations as soon as I can, and we'll be off." And so we went, first to Paris, and then by train to Marseilles, where according to Caroline, crustaceans abounded. We rented an apartment in Marseilles, which offered good access to the Mediterranean, and for me, wonderful scenes to paint.

* * *

She too was an amateur artist, as I discovered when she tried to get the details of a crab's underside on paper one day. Caroline was good, if uninspired, as a draftsman, but she was obsessed with the detail of her subjects. That was good for a biologist, but it was not art. But then what could I expect of a biologist except accuracy? Ironically my own interest in painting led to my experimenting with Impressionist techniques. Our lovemaking diminished somewhat over the next three months, not because we were bored, but because we were so intent on our creative pursuits. (In truth, we made love only two to four times a week.) We worked separately, she trying to get the details right, and I attempting to loosen up the details, like a true Impressionist. I failed for the most part, but was nevertheless pleased with some of my attempts. I said to myself, I'll keep trying till the end of the summer, and then I'll give up.

"About going back to Paris," she began one day, near the end of our stay, "I wonder if we can go back early. I'd like to get some prints of the neighborhoods I am familiar with from some of the art that I have at home." This, I learned later, was an admission by Caroline that she had other interests beyond biology in mind. I too had learned that I was not meant to be an Impressionist, much less a Dali, so we returned to Paris early.

"What are you looking for, Caroline?" I began. "Fidelity to colors, or detail of brush work?" She was looking through a series of prints propped up in an outdoor cart along the Seine.

"Both, and a lot more," she answered. She turned and looked at me. "I'm thinking of leaving biology and opening a print shop with authentic prints of Paris neighborhoods. If I can afford it, that is."

I knew that she could not afford it, having asked to share the apartment with me. So I asked her whether she'd like a loan for the initial expenses at least. My folks had given me a major gift for getting my doctorate, although it was unclear if this would be sufficient to finance a print shop whose success was uncertain.

We left the stall and began to cross the street. "Watch out!" I exclaimed as she walked into the traffic, distracted by our conversation. "They say that there are two kinds of pedestrians in Paris: the quick, and the dead. Be careful with the traffic." We resumed our conversation on the other side.

"I haven't told you this in any detail," I said, "but my family is 'filthy rich', as many people call them. They live in Wisconsin, and my father is company vice president of a prominent maker of paper goods. He's a sharp businessman, much as you are, and I think you'll like him. But I'd have to discuss with him the possibility of offering you a loan."

We entered a shop and Caroline again slowly sorted through a large number of prints, one by one, judging the colors and the texture of the brushwork, the size and framing (where they were framed at all instead of being wrapped in cellophane). She bought nothing that day, but instead visited museums to compare prints with the originals. She occasionally inquired about the possibility of opening a branch store for the Parisian shops in New Haven. This came to nothing, but at least she tried. By the time we had spent a full week in Paris, it was time to go.

"We'll talk further about our plans when we are on the plane," I said. I was pleased with her turn to art. As we left the taxi and entered the airport, I was happy to be leaving France. I had learned a lot about myself and Caroline during our time there. It seemed that our futures were highly uncertain, but I was ready for anything new. I had two more years of teaching contracted, but wished I could get out of it now that I had begun experimenting with painting. I was happy. I had spent a gorgeous summer in France with the woman I loved more than ever.

After boarding the plane, I settled down in my seat, suddenly exhausted after getting up at dawn. But Caroline was excited, as she usually was, and ready to talk nonstop. This left me no alternative but to converse with her, sleepy as I was. I don't know what came over me, but I said, "When we get married, we'll figure something out about the print shop."

"Did you just propose to me?" Caroline asked, "*Es tu bien sŭr? Seriousement?*"

"Yes, I suppose I did," I said, surprised at this turn in the conversation. "Not premeditated, I assure you, but the question is still valid. I don't know what I was thinking, but my proposal still stands." I had actually been thinking of this for some weeks, but I was characteristically afraid to ask.

"This calls for champagne at the very least!" Caroline said, and before I could do so myself, she had ordered a full bottle of champagne from the stewardess standing nearby.

"To us!" We clinked our glasses (which were made of plastic since we were flying in coach and not first class) and considered the matter settled. We then went to sleep until we arrived in New York.

* * *

"Once they meet you, my family will be impressed, mark my soul," I said, as we drove to the airport to visit the family and make the announcement of our engagement. We were heading to Wisconsin before the academic term began. I could not believe that I had proposed to Caroline on the plane, but I was glad that I had finally gotten it out.

"I look forward to meeting them," said Caroline excitedly. "I hope to make a good impression. I hope I look okay for the visit."

"Don't worry about that," I said, "you look wonderful as you always do."

On the plane to Wisconsin, we planned what to say, particularly to my father. We discussed his probable reaction, not only to the engagement, but to Caroline's plan for a print shop. Rich has he was, my father was a sharp businessman, and would take nothing for granted.

"Where were you thinking of opening the shop?" I asked.

"In some modest area that will attract, hopefully, an upscale crowd," Caroline said, with more than a touch of irony.

"I believe he'd suggest paying the rent on the shop, not buy it or anything like that. Anyway, most of these places are for rent, not for sale, since most of the shops in the districts in downtown New Haven are rentals. But I still think you may need to scale back your plans, modest as they are." I sounded like my father in saying this. I had picked up some acumen from him as a child, and I had to be realistic with Caroline.

As it turned out, my folks were mightily impressed with Caroline, who looked gorgeous as usual. She was confident at the dinner table, showing her good humor, amusing irony, and strength in conversation. After a few days, my father drew me aside and said, "You have quite a woman, son. She is a real winner! I know from talking to her that she has an eye for business." He added, "For a woman."

"Whoa there, Dad," I said, "Watch out what you say, particularly in front of Caroline."

"Sorry," my father said, "I've got to watch my language. I'm an old-school fellow, and I haven't learned PC speech yet. Nevertheless, I can spot executive ability when I see it. She wants to start a print shop in New Haven, but I don't know what her precise plans are. Have you talked about this?"

"A bit. I told her that I could take care of our expenses with my salary. And if we started small, I could pay the rent for a while out of the generous gift that you folks gave me on finishing my doctorate. Would that be okay with you?"

"A gift is a gift. Do anything you like with it."

Caroline was delighted at getting along so well with my folks, and on hearing the news about Dad's approval of our plan. We went on to hold extensive conversations with father and mother about other things, including memories of my childhood. Altogether it was a very successful visit.

* * *

When we got back to New Haven a very busy year began for me. I was occupied with my French Revolution courses at the community college but we also proceeded with Caroline's plan. We rented a shop in a run-down district of New Haven, and I spent evenings and weekends helping her refurbish the place. Seedy as it was, Caroline had an eye for design and was able to direct me in the process of making it look more than nice, tasteful, in fact. It was hard work, but well worth it. Meanwhile, I thought about my career. I decided that the vacation in France had taught me enough about painting to go professional as an artist. I would give up teaching when my contract expired next summer and help Caroline full-time with the print shop.

I discovered, to my surprise in my last year of teaching, that painting flowers in the style of Van Gogh was my métier. I remember the first time I saw his painting of *Irises* on a visit to New York, and was enthralled by them. I decided to copy the painting, and that's when it hit me. I could paint watercolors of various types of flowers: magnolias, cyclamens, asters, and a host of others. Watercolors were simple for me, so I equipped myself with the appropriate paints, paper and brushes and went to work. It was so successful that I thought of copying them with the color copier we had recently bought for the print shop and turn them into greeting cards and sell them. They sold well, but brought in little money, not enough, of course, to support the operation of the print shop. That job— ordering prints from France—fell to Caroline. After a while, to our surprise, customers slowly discovered the shop despite the rundown appearance of the adjacent storefronts. Thanks to Caroline's good taste, the shop was holding its own.

Unlike my commencement, my parents did attend our wedding the following summer. It was not large, since in spite of their wealth they did not like ostentation. If they had any concern about whether Caroline loved me for their money, it was allayed by her happy agreement to a relatively private ceremony with just our parents and close family friends at a Catholic Church near Fenway Park in Boston. Since neither of us was a big baseball fan, we were a little surprised that my father had purchased tickets for us to attend a Red Sox game on the next day. With our academic backgrounds Caroline and I researched baseball before the wedding, so that we were able to understand the game and follow the scoring. Dad brought us hot dogs and beer, and we enjoyed ourselves even though this experience was far removed from out interest in art and painting.

And then, in the middle of the eight inning, it happened. The band began playing "Sweet Caroline." Dad quietly clinked his beer bottle against Caroline's, and mine, and mother's. It reminded me of our plastic champagne glass toast the day I inadvertently asked Caroline to marry me on the plane trip back from Paris.

Sweet Caroline
Good times never seemed so good

We of course touched hands when the lyrics prompted us. My father looked very pleased with his Red Sox game surprise.

I did not teach that fall, working at the print shop instead, which was becoming more and more successful. My father, we learned, was tracking its fortunes quietly. Always a businessman, he waited until the shop succeeded before he decided to supplement our rather modest wedding gift—and what a supplement it turned out to be! We were now able to afford moving the shop to a much better, upscale domain in another part of town. I continued painting in my spare time, and my Impressionist-inspired landscapes and floral watercolors were also beginning to attract customers.

My discontent at this time in my life was that I was beginning to have a wish for children. We had a few words about this desire of mine, but Caroline was always reluctant because of the work involved in the print shop, even after we moved it to the better location. With my usual reticence I was uncomfortable bringing up the subject.

One night after dinner we were enjoying a cappuccino in our living room when Caroline told me about a problem she had been dealing with. One of her print suppliers in France had mistakenly charged her twice for postage after a large shipment. She was relieved that the problem had finally been resolved. "So you'll be happy to hear that I'm finally off the bill," she said in a very soft tone of voice, taking a sip of her coffee and giving me a sly smile.

"I'm glad to hear it," I told her. I was a little puzzled because the conversation did not have the usual briskness of business discussions with Caroline.

She burst out laughing. "You don't get it, do you?" She laughed again. "I'm not off the bill—I'm off the Pill!"

I was stunned. "I am delighted, not to mention excited! You have your own curious way of telling me about such things!" I suddenly remembered that she had brought up kissing and living together in similar ways.

"There's more," she said, winking at me. Then she cleared her throat and began softly singing the first stanza of "Sweet Caroline":

> Where it began
> I can't begin to knowin'
> But then I know it's growing strong
> Was in the spring
> And spring became a summer
> Who'd believe you'd come along

"You mean?" I was stunned again. She nodded.

"Are you sure?" I asked. She assured me that I had it right.

"Three months without a period, I am certain. And a pregnancy test. I didn't want to tell you until I was quite sure. It's never good to report false positives."

"That's why you stopped drinking martinis a couple months ago! I thought it was on account of stress." She nodded and reached over and kissed me on the cheek.

Now it was my turn. I put one arm around her shoulder, and touched her hand with the other. Then I softly crooned:

Sweet Caroline
Good times never seemed so good

Caroline suddenly shot upright. "Pardon me," she said, "but I have to go throw up. Morning sickness, you know."

MAYA

I have to introduce you to my friend, Maya. The relationship with Maya evolved over several years while I was a student working with George Forrest (who ultimately won the Nobel prize in medicine). Maya was a fellow graduate student in biology during this period and I got to know her rather well. Being the only two graduate students in Forrest's lab at the time, we were naturally thrown together, and I was happy to have her company. She had long hair, with narrow, mysterious eyes. When she smiled her eyes narrowed further, and her high cheekbones make her look faintly Asian. She had a purposeful way of walking, and I could tell when she approached me, even from behind. She was supremely articulate and witty in a way that reminded me of Dorothy Parker in one of her less inebriated periods.

She was, however, subject to periods of depression. I became involved trying to help at these times, and it seemed to work somewhat. It appeared she needed me to talk to; and it felt good to be of help. But for the life of me I could not figure out what was wrong with her. Instead of getting to the heart of her problems, we talked idly, humorously, of superficial topics, which seemed to help because they addressed her built-in sense of humor. I wondered whether this was a mask to hide her underlying problems, but I never asked. We went for coffee that extended well past the time we had set. Suffice it to say I was slightly scared of her at first, so I hesitated to open up to her. The fact that we were the only two graduate students in Forrest's lab at the time threw us together more than I would've liked. But I never said so, to her or anyone else.

While I'm at it, I should say that my wife and I were having problems of our own, and I was not sure where they originated. In fact, I didn't know until later how we got into them to the extent we did. But get into them we did. It started as a sudden preoccupation in the third year of our marriage on my wife's part that remained unexplained, and remained so for the duration of our marriage. Was she having an affair with one her fellow graduate students? Or did it have to do with her studies in advanced math? When I asked my wife what was bothering her, it sounded like an accusation for which I felt sorry She said it was the stress of her studies, but I didn't believe her. I was afraid to ask further, and, putting on a cheerful exterior, went about my business seemingly untroubled by my concerns. But in the meantime, in private, and in unguarded moments, I became increasingly moody myself. The marriage didn't last long; it was over by the end of the third year, when I was already working in the Forrest lab. I learned later, she was having an affair with a person she had known since high school.

This left me with Maya, who as I say, was attractive, funny, and moody at the same time. She reminded me powerfully of my wife, but her good humor (when she was in a good humor, which she often was) turned out to be a blessing.

"What are you doing? I mean now." She would ask.

"Taking notes on my last experiment. I mean now," I would answer.

"Let's have some coffee. I too mean now," she would reply.

"Let's not. I'm busy."

"Aww. So I'll be left alone, without companionship, abandoned like a ship at sea, without a rudder." Maya spoke with an air of exaggerated disappointment, smiling all the while.

"I hope you drown in an ocean of coffee." Then I relented. "Okay, okay. I'll go for coffee, reluctant as I am." I said this with an air of relief as though I did not care about the experiment I was taking notes on.

This kind of repartee was common between us because in my heart of hearts, I wanted distraction. And what sort of person could distract me better?

As my relationship with my wife became increasingly tense, I warmed to Maya as she in turn became more relaxed and funnier. At the time my experiments were going quite well and I felt there was more time to waste.

"Why don't we go to a movie?" she asked one afternoon. Somehow she had sensed that things were not going well at home and here she was asking me for a date. This was bold of her since I'd never opened up to her about my marital difficulties. I was therefore stumped for an answer. It was early evening, my wife had recently moved out, and I was still feeling down. After a few moments I asked her, "What were you thinking of seeing?"

"'*Casablanca*'" she answered. "I've never seen it and it's here only one more day."

"You're on," I said.

When we got back from the movie, she invited me into her room at the Graduate Center. I was surprised at how messy it looked, with books strewn about and signs of work. It was clear that if she had a partner or a lover, he was a forgiving fellow. From the look of the room, it appeared that she was working all the time, maybe even more at home than at work. She offered me a drink, which I accepted gladly, and we talked about the movie. *Casablanca* was good. I had seen it before, and I enjoyed it just as much this time. To my surprise, Maya seemed filled with pleasure at our evening together. As I got ready to leave, she kissed me for my having accepted her invitation. One thing led to another, and we started fooling around as they say. She invited me to have another drink, which I accepted without hesitation. I must've enjoyed the movie even more than she did, given how elated I too felt. I was tempted to go further, but thought better of it. As a result I went home somewhat—only somewhat—satisfied.

So began a relationship with Maya that I never anticipated and of which I felt terrified at the outset. We didn't get into a truly close relationship until I had relaxed to some extent after my divorce was final. At first I was my usual joking self, full of repartee. Did she have no other partners? I had no idea and I felt naïve as soon as I asked myself this. Her regular appearance in the lab at night and her suggesting the movie minimized my doubts at least for the moment. One night, it went from caresses to actual intercourse, and I wanted more. She was willing, eager, in fact. This put a sense of danger in play, and I liked that, to my surprise.

In the meantime, I became more and more fond of Maya. And I might add, she of me. For a time, I didn't ask her about other lovers. I hinted around about this a bit when she was in a good mood, which was often now. I attributed this to the increasing ease and rewards of sex. Nevertheless she remained opaque on the subject. I was troubled by her reluctance to say anything about her past. There was little doubt that she was not a virgin, so I tried to forget the whole thing and go on from there. The Graduate Center had no parietal rules, so I slept at Maya's place more frequently.

* * *

One night I got up the courage to ask Maya about her rounds of depression when I first met her. She had been happy as a clam since we had begun sleeping with one another, but now and again she returned to her depressive mood. It was as if her previous concerns had surfaced again. We were in bed, and feeling close, so I chose this time to broach the subject.

"I hoped you would never ask," she finally said dryly. "But it had to come sometime, and it might as well be now." She turned in the bed, wrapping herself in a sheet. "It's a long story, and if you're willing, I can give you the long version or the short version."

"I might as well have the long version, since I've been meaning to ask for a long time." At last, I was going to hear something about her past, and I waited in fascination.

"I was fifteen going on sixteen years old when my mother married my stepfather, whose name was Harold," she began. "Did you know that my father died in a car crash?" she asked in passing. "That's another long story, but I can't go into that now. Anyway, I didn't realize how handsome my stepfather was, because I never met him before the wedding. They got married after a whirlwind romance in Las Vegas, and I couldn't go because I was in school at the time. He was somewhat younger than my mother, and he was attractive in a cute sort of way. Since at this stage of my life my hormones were getting the better of me, I sort of led him on." She breathed deeply, as though to rest for a moment before she went further.

"And?" I said.

"So, he began to see more and more of me while my mother was at work, and even at home in my room when she was there. When I realized that he was obsessed with me, I took it as a sign of danger, and I stopped leading him on. I was embarrassed to realize that I was competing with *my own mother*. She was attractive in her own right, and I started to leave both of them alone hoping Harold would turn back to her. I never slept with him or did anything too out of bounds. But I looked attractive to him, something I seemed not to be able to help, and so nothing changed."

"You can't help being attractive, Maya." I told her.

"Anyway," she went on, "when I realized his obsession had gotten the better of him, I was really scared and spent a lot of time away from home. It was easy, since I had school, to which I applied myself more earnestly. That's probably why I wound up here at Harvard. Just after I turned sixteen, I came back from school one day and discovered Harold had committed suicide by hanging himself in the attic. I felt completely responsible for this tragic act, and never got over it. It seems that Mother suspected the worst of my behavior in the early stages of my relationship with Harold. She therefore blamed me for the suicide and moved to California without me within two years. That," she concluded, "explains my moroseness when you first met me." To my surprise, she began crying. A long wail followed by blubbering. I didn't know what to do, so I kept silent until she was finished.

When she could speak again she said, "I was surprised when the legalities were over that Harold had left me over three quarters of a million dollars in his will. I could draw on it after I turned eighteen, and the terms of the will were not contestable, according to the lawyers. Harold must've owned interest in one of the casinos. My mother was truly pissed, and that explains why she moved away after I became eighteen. She knew I could take care of myself, and since he left her an equal amount she was okay too. But I still felt both guilty and burdened by the terms of Harold's will. It shows that he felt guilty as hell, even though I was the one that started the whole thing and was responsible. And I still feel guilty that his will allows me to live so comfortably—you notice I don't have a roommate or any other encumbrances." I was glad to hear the last word of that sentence, needless to say.

"I've never told anyone about Harold's suicide, even my best friends in high school and college. I've always kept it inside me like a deep, dark secret. Even my very few other lovers never learned about my past. But now that I've told you the whole story, I feel much better." She took a deep breath, and then she smiled at me. "It's been cathartic," she said. "Thank you for listening."

I hoped I had gotten the whole story and that there weren't more secrets. I had certainly learned a lot about Maya, and her past. "Do you have any contact at all with your mother?"

"No," she said sadly. "I tried. I even hired a detective so I could find her and apologize to her. But mother was absolutely not open to further contact by phone or letter."

"It must have been hard on you all these years." I couldn't imagine cutting off contact with my mother, particularly if we were connected by the tragic events that Maya had described.

"Yes," she said simply. And with that, she unwrapped herself from the sheet and gave herself to me with grateful ardor.

* * *

After that night and the copious revelations she had offered, I knew that I was deeply in love with Maya. "Your turn," she said, lifting her eyebrows. We were having coffee in the laboratory, and no one else was around.

"What do you mean, 'your turn'?"

"To tell me about your past," Maya said with a frown. "I've told you a great deal that I haven't told anyone, but I know little about you. Except for your experiments. For instance, how did your marriage end? You've mentioned you were divorced, but you never told me how it ended."

"Well," I began hesitantly, "I met Lisa in graduate school, and we had a whirlwind romance. I married her after a short engagement, and this seemed to be the beginning of a wonderful relationship. As Bogart said to Louis at the end of *Casablanca,* 'Louis, I think this is the beginning of a beautiful relationship.'"

"Friendship," Maya interrupted. "He said 'I think this is the beginning of a beautiful friendship'."

I laughed. "You're right. I should have listened to him and started with a friendship rather than with a whirlwind romance."

I took a moment before going on because I realized that we were going to get into tricky territory when I went on with my story.

"Anyway, all went well for the first two years until I began to notice some suspicious goings on that I couldn't figure out. I found out later that she had slept repeatedly with a fellow graduate student whom she had known previously. That was why things turned ugly during the last year of our marriage. It was all over as quickly as it had begun. End of story."

Maya closed her eyes and looked bleak. "I suppose that's the story my mother tells people, except she'd have to add that it was her own daughter who was the culprit who caused her husband's suicide."

I reached over and patted her arm. "Maya you were very young and you had lost your father in a way that surely felt traumatic to you. That might have had something to do with your behavior toward Harold."

She frowned. This had clearly not occurred to her before.

I went on. "It also sounds as though Harold maybe couldn't help himself either. You were a minor and he should certainly have backed off. But his feelings…Well, anyway, it's over."

"Except for my mother," she said abjectly.

"Your mother's grief is certainly understandable, but if she blames you she's very wrong." I'd been thinking about this and realizing that there was another whole angle to this business that Maya needed to consider. "If your mother suspected something going on she had an obligation to confront Harold and you about it. She would even have been obliged to report him to the police, I suspect."

"I don't want to hear that, "Maya said, "because it doesn't help me deal with my guilt. That's why I've never gone to a therapist—because I knew that's what they'd say and it would only make me feel more guilty."

We were both silent for a few minutes, trying to thread our way through the complexities of this situation. Finally I said, "Maya, I think you need to stop thinking about this whole thing in terms of blame, and just accept it as an unfortunate all-around tragedy."

Maya looked at me. "But you blame your wife, don't you?"

My answer surprised even me. "I did, until you told me your story. But it made me realize that not everyone can control their feelings of love or sex or whatever, and that includes my wife. Maybe it was better for her to go with a new partner. You know, 'the beginning of a beautiful relationship.'"

"Friendship," she said. A small smile came back to her face.

"Friendship," I agreed. "And maybe it was better for me to have the demise of my marriage let me start 'the beginning of a beautiful friendship' too," I looked at her fondly as I said this.

"How did the divorce affect your income?" Maya asked.

I was surprised at this turn in the conversation. "No children, no child support. And no alimony on either side. Assets split down the middle."

"So you're okay?"

"Well," I said, "with the combination of a small allowance from my folks, a fellowship and a tutorial job at Dunster house, I'm set for room and board and I can support myself in a reasonable way." She had never visited me in Dunster house since the lab was closer to her room in the Graduate Center. And because it would appear unseemly for tutors to have guests—especially female—for overnight visits.

"I'm not ready to get married, but I'm tempted," she said. "You've been so supportive that I can't thank you enough. Let's give it time before we make any mistakes."

Another surprise. I hesitated only for a second before I said, "That sounds like a conditional proposal." And then, "I accept."

* * *

After getting our Ph.D.'s in one more year, we were married. Maya's thesis had not been satisfying, and to no one's surprise, she dropped out of science to satisfy her ambitions as a writer. I had mentioned that she was witty in a Dorothy Parker sort of way, and she exploited this to the hilt. She was successful in this from the start, writing two moderately successful romance novels. In addition, she was the life of every party we attended. She completely dropped her previous moroseness for good. I myself was eventually recruited from my position at Stanford to take Forrest's place at Harvard, where I had a moderately successful career.

Maya was happy, succeeding in her writing well into her sixties. We had no children, which made it easy for me to work in the lab. Maya eventually received two writing awards, one quite prestigious. And her books made money for her so she could maintain her finances which ultimately outstripped mine.

We never returned to the subject of her mother, Harold, or his bequest to Maya. And because she remained happy and never alluded to it again, I was happy too. It's remarkable how two brief conversations can change two lives.

Maya died in my arms, close to our fortieth wedding anniversary. My grief left me stunned and almost paralyzed. But after grieving a year or more, I began to think of Maya again and how happy I was to have had her. It was the memory of Maya that gave me new hope and a new life and allowed me to marry again in my seventies. I was going to be blessed to die an emotionally rich man.

STILL LIFE

The doctor at Pittsfield General said Lucia's eyes were open the moment she emerged from Anna's womb. From the start, Lucia looked at everything closely, holding her hand motionless inspecting her little fingers, feeling her blanket as she brought it to her eyes. She pressed closely to her mother, scrutinizing the tiny moles and hairs, the freckles and folds of Anna's neck as she lay in her mother's arms, even at two months. Lucia soon crawled about, frowning at her surroundings, her world an elusive challenge. When she cruised as a toddler, she pulled herself up to see what was on tables, reach for them, and look at them solemnly. She paid little attention to her parents then, but she accepted their help as they showed her the small things she could not get for herself. Anna and Harold saw Lucia grow and learn, relieved to discover that she was not autistic. Nevertheless, they looked with concern and wonder at Lucia's intense preoccupation with the visible world.

The many drawings she made when she was two showed rapid improvement. With crayons and soon with hard black and colored pencils, she filled sheets and sheets of paper and sketch books, not with stick figures and faces with two dots and a smile, but smooth circles for her beads and balls, a well-formed fuzzy animal for her stuffed bear, green leaves with veins, and once her father asleep in his chair. By her fifth birthday, she would sit on the back steps of the house, sharpening her pencils almost angrily for greater exactness.

She brushed her blonde hair from her eyes, nodding over close work on her pad, pursing her lips as she perfected each line. Her drawings choked the page, from the distant branches and rooftops to the rough bark of nearby trees, the textures growing out of the paper almost as real as nature had made them. She became increasingly dissatisfied with color, using it only for blue backgrounds for sky, tilting the pencil low for even application of the color before using the sharp black pencils to draw over it. Rarely satisfied, she would tear the page with a single motion from its spiral binding and set it aside, starting anew with the same scene.

Lucia's penciled scenes became dead and gray, as devoid of perspective as they were profuse in detail, one thing laid atop another in a density of lines and shading that omitted nothing. She raged as she tried vainly to include her shoes in a scene that started at the top with a distant telephone pole. She rendered the background with the same crisp detail as the grass blades and spiderwebs and tattered awning and the flagstones leading up to her feet. No people, birds, caterpillars or any living, moving thing appeared in her work. She said she couldn't catch things that changed as she drew. Even breezes that moved the branches of the trees made her pause until they abated. She stopped and destroyed her work if she felt she could not take up where she left off. And nowhere was glass to be seen.

"Lucy dear, can I have this drawing? Don't throw it away."

"Mother, give it to me. No!"

"They said they might print something of yours in the paper. I can write about it too." Anna had a column in the *Pittsfield Ledger*.

"No!"

"Lucy! Stop or you'll tear it!" Anna let it go and Lucia balled up the paper after tearing it in two.

Anna, chastened as always, continued to encourage Lucia. She regretted that Lucia had given up colored pencils and pastels. A week later, she asked Lucia, "Why don't you try watercolors again? You tried them once. They'd make your pictures much nicer."

"No, they won't."

"Try it, her mother said."

"No," Lucia said, "they're messy. Leave me alone."

"I'm sorry, Lucy, but you won't learn if you don't try."

Lucia never succumbed to her mother's praise and tore her drawings twice across and sat on them as soon as she had torn them from her pad. Lucia sought privacy, slipping outdoors before breakfast, keeping her door closed in the mornings, hiding the few works she didn't destroy. Always she kept looking about, absorbing every detail of her surroundings, sometimes collecting leaves and stones and dandelions to work with in her room. She learned as she grew to parry questions about her drawings with a polite smile, dissembling after her worrisome silences at meals and her aloofness from other children at play. When pressed in earnest about why she was so intent about her drawing, she reddened and said she didn't know, or she couldn't tell.

"We may have an artist," her father said, "but she's completely obsessive. We should have done something earlier about her. We've disagreed too long on this, Annie. We've got to do something."

"Harold, for heaven's sake, give her a chance, she's just entered school. She's like me when I started writing dumb stories at her age. And I'm glad I did."

"She's not doing what she likes. She's possessed, like a gambler. We should have gotten a house nearer town. More life, more children."

"She'll meet children in school. She's in an art class."

"She hates the art class from what she says. You know that."

"They're letting her alone now, like we do. She's calming down."

"Even if she is, how is she going to get her talent in gear? She can't learn much doing what she's always done. None of her stuff is good enough for her. That's why she won't try anything new."

"Harold, let's just see how she does in school. It's too early to force anything. I only wish she took better care of herself."

"She's haunted, Annie. I don't know what's going to happen to her. I couldn't believe she hated the Norman Rockwell things in Stockbridge. She was actually scared of the pictures!"

"She's an artist. She'll find her way. And she'd be beautiful if she only kept her hair combed and had some pride in her work. Loosen up, Harold. I can talk to her even if you can't."

Lucia grew into a slender ten-year-old with long blond hair and huge blue eyes, deeply set beneath her brow. She looked like a Scandinavian princess, with a purposeful jaw and fine lips. But her inattention to her blouses, jeans, and moccasins, which she wore without socks, marred her daily appearance. She always worked with cold passion, her drawings little episodes in a life struggle. She softened up a little when Anna and Harold put her in private lessons with Ivo Srb, a sympathetic and admiring teacher. By the time she was eleven, the tutoring had made an impression. The break came when Ivo Srb, frustrated by Lucia's refusal to work with watercolors, introduced her to acrylics, a more exact and less exacting medium. Lucia's work bloomed, and her teacher stood aside as Lucia became even more proficient than he himself.

It was Srb who first made Anna and Harold fully aware that Lucia refused to depict glass or water. "She says it warps things, makes the light wrong," Srb said.

"Why? It's as real as anything else."

"Frankly," the teacher said, "she's afraid of glass and bottles and marbles. But she's fascinated by them. I don't understand it either. She's afraid too to use her imagination. In fact, I'd hate to be around when she sees her first Dali."

Lucia confined herself to drawing outdoors, since it required little equipment and because acrylics dried too fast in the open air. She attracted a few curious girlfriends. To them, her drawings were so vivid and executed so boldly that the friends became quiet as Lucia worked. Lucia, with muted concern, turned on them with a cold stare if they said much or came too close, much as she did with her parents. She cultivated friendships only with the gentlest of them, girls her age she could complain to quietly about her parents.

She befriended only one boy, Ashton, a fellow student of Ivo Srb, who was a year older. Ashton expressed a genuine, good-humored admiration for Lucia's work. He often walked with her to the outskirts of the town, their sketch pads under their arms. On rare occasions, he carried her box and easel for her, but most often they simply drew in the woods. One fall, he sat near her, resting with his pad against his legs as he leaned against an oak. The autumn colors had come early, in early October, and red and gold leaves from the maples littered the forest floor. Lucia sat cross-legged on a bed of moss, in the shade, drawing. Ashton glanced at Lucia's work.

"Looking at your stuff, I'm ready to give up."

"What?" Lucia looked up, pencil poised.

"I said I could never do that kind of work, every leaf."

"Is there anything wrong with it?"

"No, just so fast, like you're trying to make a photo. You'd at least get the colors with a camera."

"So?"

"So why don't you try something simpler, maybe color. I'll lend you my pencil set."

"I'm past that."

"I guess, but I'll bring my camera for you next time."

"Very funny."

"Sorry. Didn't mean to tick you off."

"I'm just a little sensitive. I can't get it right even with a No. 3 pencil."

"I just thought maybe it's too right."

"Is that bad?"

"Like Ivo says, there's truth and then there's beauty."

"Same thing, Ashton. We talked about all that before. Don't bug me."

At Christmas that year she had her first period, spotting lightly in December, bleeding more the next month. Anna had prepared Lucia for this earlier, and encouraged her to think of it as a happy new year. Anna, peeking one morning into Lucia's little studio area in her bedroom, was shocked to find an acrylic, an image of Lucia's stained blue panties lying on the floor beside her bed. The image was so real, the folds so true, the red so right, the nap of the green carpet so vivid that she reached with fascination and faint disgust to touch it. Her mother said nothing of this to Harold or Lucia. She had forced herself for some time to accept that Lucia was in charge of her artistic life, not to be goaded or guided. Leave it to Ivo, she thought, a lucky find in a small city. Two months before, Lucia had made a huge scene, screaming at her father when he looked at some paintings as he helped her take them for storage in the shed next to the garage. Lucia's growing collection of paintings, the few she saved, began to fill the shed, secured with a padlock she had bought herself. The paintings she destroyed sometimes littered the back lawn, cut up and defaced beyond recognition, ready to be collapsed and hauled away with the trash. Every week she and Anna bought more paper pads, canvas board, stretched canvasses and other supplies from the art store in town. At least, Anna said to herself one day, she keeps up with school work. It's probably where she gets her rest.

Lucia went over to oil paints, having found acrylics "impossible," especially outdoors. Glass and water still frustrated her with their distortions of background and light. In fact, she had spent two weeks once at home several years before secretly trying, in vain, to paint a satisfactory acrylic of a ceramic bowl on her green rug in the sunlight from the window. She was now fifteen, increasingly proficient in her small studio keeping a tidy palette, mixing colors with care. She cleaned her many brushes carefully, making exacting choices for each application. She used subtle colors for underpainting and backgrounds on her canvases, seeing in advance how they would support the final image. She filled and textured small areas, whose exquisite edges replaced the fine penciled outlines of her earlier work. She chose her scenes more carefully, scenes that were simpler and demanded much less detail to render them arresting to the viewer. Her close-up images were never arranged, but simply chosen, whether it was bread on polished, fine-grained wood, or the fabric and aglet of a shoelace, or the muted brown shine of a dead crow's beak, a lucky find one day in the woods.

In the next year, a disturbance crept into her vision. The world seemed to take on motion and odd rhythms. Just at the edge of her vision, the trees writhed, the walls bulged slightly and sighed. Indeed, from her childhood, huge summer clouds expanding slowly in midsummer afternoons before a rain had always threatened her. Did the world have a secret life beyond the winds and creeping vines and nocturnal animals? Had her vision improved even further, she asked herself. Looked at directly and steadily, the faint, odd motions around her stopped, but resumed in the corner of her eye when she looked away.

She asked some of her hangers-on if they saw this, almost insisting to them that they must. None shared Lucia's perception and turned from her in wonder when she wouldn't let it go. Only Ashton took the matter seriously, saying he sometimes saw this when he got up too suddenly or looked away from a bright light. But never in the corner of his eye, like Lucia said. Don't worry about it, he said. Lucia stopped asking, but felt danger in her inability now to ignore these instabilities or render them properly. Her drawings and paintings became smaller, close-ups, miniatures depicting flowers and stones and dead insects, anything she could hold in her hand, anything that would stay still as she worked. She captured the stillness in small things, all things except glass, avoiding as always windows, clear bottles, glasses of water. They shimmered even when she looked at them directly.

Ashton improved rapidly in his own work, now painting mainly deft watercolors. He became closer to Lucia, happy to be with her, seeing her beauty not only in her work but also in her disheveled person. But he was too shy to move further into her affections, such as they might be.

"Ashton," she said one day, giving a theatrical shudder, "I'm afraid. It's like everything is moving in on me. Things move, but I know they don't. Sometimes they disappear and come back a little closer. Sort of like a creepy movie."

"To tell you the truth, Lucy, your work is getting more life. It seems more interesting. You should just go on with it."

"You never liked my stuff. But I'm doing it my way."

"I do like it, always have. I'm saying whatever you're seeing, that may be why I like your paintings more now."

"It's not real, though."

"What you paint is what you see. Just do it. No one's gonna complain."

Lucia's mother and father remained circumspect, but always encouraged her to continue, to improve, to get more instruction. Lucia showed her parents her best work occasionally, and they knew by that time that she would be famous if she continued trying to satisfy her insatiable quest for realism. In fact by now Lucia, with Ashton's encouragement, had uncannily incorporated some of the impressions of movement that she kept seeing. The objects in the painting were indescribable in words, their shadows rendered with extraordinary fidelity, all of nature's tricks of light reduced to a luminous, two-dimensional vision. She painted with diminishing frustration what she saw. She even began to take on bottles and water with a pride in her abilities, much as she had dared long ago to use color. Ivo Srb now abandoned his effort to widen her range, to try slight impressionistic flourishes, and simply let her deepen her own style. He could help her only technically with the choice of brushes or color mix. She had conquered the world around her and smiled now as her parents and her few friends gazed in awe at her facility.

Lucia's mother received an amaryllis bulb for Christmas when Lucia turned fifteen. Soon after the bulb was planted in a pot, two pale green shoots poked through the soil and grew by the day. Yes, Lucia thought, they moved, thrust themselves upward slowly and fattened when she was not looking. Days later, the shoots had separated into straplike leaves surrounding a thick flower stem. The stem bore a large bud that over a single night opened into a huge red blossom, its supple corolla hungry for light and attention. It shimmered in the morning sun, its stamens and yellow anthers thrust out into the air. Lucia shuddered with wonder and took the plant in its pot to her studio to paint it before it changed. She could hardly hold her brush steady to the canvas as she captured the living plant, throbbing in the corner of her eye as she turned back to the picture. It was a glimpse of great beauty, transcending the truth she had tried to capture for so many years. She felt her body contract with a gush of energy that would transform all her work thereafter. Her breath caught in her throat, and she smiled, victorious.

* * *

Lucia now showed her work in local galleries and shops. Pittsfield businesses asked for her work to sell or to adorn their premises. Word got around in western Massachusetts that a prodigy had come into her own. "Norma Rockwell," the *Pittsfield Ledger* announced, a sobriquet Lucia and her mother hated and could not suppress, even though Anna was a writer for the paper. At least, Anna knew, her daughter now scorned rather than feared the work of the Stockbridge master. Her parents did not have to persuade Lucia to ignore the attention she attracted. Lucia worked without interruption as her parents took care of the practicalities of their daughter's renown, her obsession now her career. Her parents arranged, with the financial help of the Pittsfield Rotary, to send her to the Eastman School for more training. She entered the year after Ashton went away to college. Unable to try or to adapt to other genres and media, she left after a single year. She retired to her home in Pittsfield to paint, to paint, and to paint, never tiring of the utterly familiar, a reality she rendered into magic for the rest of the world.

Trained artists referred to her work as ultrareal, pointing to the almost invisible nimbus surrounding objects, subtle elements few other artists had ever captured. When she was twenty, a New York cable television host interviewed Lucia, with one of her landscapes in view. She sat by the painting, squirming, trying to keep her eyes off the camera lens with its uncanny reflection of the studio lights.

"Lucia, just how do you go about that?"

"What? This painting? Just look closely and paint what I see."

"Artists say that, but can you say something about the process?"

"Well, there's nothing wrong, is there?"

"No, but somehow it looks like you could walk into it."

"It's not magic. I just choose what I paint. And use the right brushes and pigments and take enough time. Like artists everywhere. Nothing special."

"But you never paint or even draw people. Or animals."

"No. They move."

Lucia's parents, now at ease with their daughter's reputation, sought a more prominent outlet for her work. Ashton returned to Pittsfield the summer after his graduation and told Lucia and her parents he had gotten a job in New York, working as an assistant in a gallery. He persuaded his employer that Lucia's paintings might find a following there. In six months, the gallery became the exclusive outlet for the many paintings stored in the shed by the garage of her parents' house. Her parents guarded her income and several years later used it to buy an old farm house with a barn for her in the country nearby on a two-lane road. They oversaw, with Lucia and Ashton, a remodeling of the barn as a studio and storage space for her work. They planted oleanders along the front, put in a graveled driveway under the maples and painted the elm-shaded house white, like all the houses in the area. The barn became a studio and storage place for many paintings that did not go to New York. Ashton and Harold restored the rich red paint on the outside of the weathered structure. The entire compound disguised the supreme work that went on inside; no signs or notice attracted the few tourists that motored by. Gradually Pittsfield made less of her. She thought of Pittsfield now as a past world, even though it remained her home. Even people who knew her in earlier times left her respectfully to her work.

Lucia never attended a showing in New York, reluctant to meet the buyers of her work, saying truthfully that she was busy with new projects. Ashton, now a gentle twenty-five-year old, came each month or two to bring her paintings from Pittsfield to New York. He said to clients he was proud to know Lucia, blushing as he described their chaste friendship.

The owner encouraged him in this role as a curious asset in the business.

The next years suggested, in a subtle way, that she may have reached a peak shortly after she had opened in New York. Comparison showed a slight fading of the qualities that brought gasps from those who looked at her work the first time. She worked every day till she could hardly see, capturing as best she could the entire world, putting it on canvas or paper, working fast before it escaped by a change of the light. She again became doubtful she could catch nature's secrets adequately, trying over and over to experience the feeling that the Christmas amaryllis had imparted to her so strongly years ago. Her hair again lost its luster, and her fine lips, once gently held open with dignity as she painted, became strained at the corners. People and classmates from the old days saw in her, when they saw her at all, the obsessed child they once knew. She spent more time on miniatures, confining herself often to the barn.

Ashton visited his parents, now ailing, more often. He would come in his panel truck, usually on a Friday mid-afternoon. He always visited Lucia, whether or not she had more work for the gallery. She became closer to him again, reliving their days in the woods, the two sometimes going out to their old locations. He still seemed daunted by her separateness, her attention to what she saw, and by her growing reputation. As he told her of the popularity of her work and the reactions of buyers and people visiting the gallery, she became quiet, embarrassed by Ashton's accounts. Over these weekends, Ashton helped her stretch canvasses, repair and clean up easels, hang paintings and fix lights in the barn.

"Ashton, you're so much help to me out here. Daddy can't do it anymore. I have to thank you."

"I hope I can help whenever I get up here."

"Don't you want to enjoy New York on the weekends?"

"I'm a loner too. You know me. I come here to rest and see my parents. The city's not my kind of place."

"Well I'm glad you're here."

"So am I. I love seeing your work in progress. I always learn a lot."

By May of the last year, the last of all, Lucia had not offered paintings to show for five months. It was a long time, given her pace. Ashton came home for two weeks after a busy season in the city and looked in first on Lucia. He turned into the graveled driveway as the afternoon sun shone from a deep blue sky through the new leaves of the maples, tiny insects swarming in the light. Lucia's house stood modestly set back, protected from the road by the unkempt oleander hedge, now taller than Ashton. The elm near the house had grown more robust in the seven years since she moved there, shadowing the roof, its branches tangling with those of the old oaks between the house and the barn. The barn's weathered red walls had acquired a more natural look that revealed again its prominent wood grain.

This time, Lucia was not working in the barn. Ashton found her sitting on the two-seat glider, unmoving, on the porch of the house. She held a lilac before her face, looking intently at it. She looked toward him with a faint smile as she set the flower in her lap. He came up the walk and stood at the bottom of the steps. After a moment, he smiled, mounted to the porch and sat beside her.

"I hope I'm not interrupting anything," he said as he damped the swing of the glider.

"No, I'm glad you came, Ashton. You make me calm, like in the old days."

"Like the old days? You weren't so calm then."

"Well, I didn't get so tired then. I only work till early afternoon now."

"Every day?"

"Pretty much. I'm doing more work in the barn where the light is better."

"Well, I'd love to see any new work you have. I still wish I knew how you do it. Even how you live this way. When I came up just now, you looked like one of your still lifes."

"Thank you."

"Anyway, what have you got this time?"

"Not much, and I don't think they're much good. Three small ones."

"Can I see them?"

"Okay, I guess. Come to the barn."

He followed her on the dirt path over to the barn. They entered through a small door beside the large main sliding door, the latter secured with a rusty lock. Lucia switched on the lights attached to the beams of the hayloft above. The smell of turpentine was fainter than on Ashton's previous visits. Even though they had come in from a bright afternoon, Ashton was almost blinded by the lights. He looked away to the right wall, seeing several small paintings, all three of them depicting closely observed rocks lying on a board. As he turned to Lucia, he asked if they were the ones. He gazed at her in shock. Lucia was weeping silently, copiously.

"Lucy! What's the matter?"

"I'm sorry. Ashton, I'm going blind." She picked a rag from an easel and wiped her eyes.

"No!" He stood still, rooted like one of the oaks outside.

"Retinopathy." She strangled on the word. "Autoimmune retinopathy. Soon."

"That can't be true, Lucy, you're still painting."

"The doctor's right, Ashton…I'm…I'm sorry."

Ashton said nothing as he moved closer to her. Slowly, he put his right arm around her shoulders. He looked into her face as her hair fell over her brimming eyes. For the first time, he embraced her fully, attaining now what he had never felt possible. Her long body sagged as she turned against his chest like a loose-limbed doll, her arms over his shoulders. All the beautiful canvasses that had stood between them so long slid away. As he kissed her cheeks, she clung to his shoulder, crying now in a soft, choking whimper. After a minute, she stood fully upright, still embracing him. The lights lit her face, softened by her emotions. Ashton could see every hair and tear-track and crease of her beautiful lips. He brushed her hair aside and looked into her huge, failing eyes, a place he had never been before.

"Lucy, you are so alone. How can I help?"

"I'm sorry, Ashton. I'm dead if I can't paint. There's nothing."

"There is. What can I do?"

"I didn't ever know what to do with you, Ashton. Be with me?"

"What do your parents know?"

"They know I have a problem. But not how big. They're too good to me. Those are my last paintings. I'm dying."

"Your mother and father have to know. I'll tell them. I know them. Let me."

"Ashton. All right. Don't leave me."

Ashton stayed with her that night, entangled in her long limbs, pressing her to him in the dark, both of them finding breathless beauty in what they could not see.

The whole world now trembled before her as she stood in the mornings, greeting the sun and its warmth as she always had. As the next few months went by, color drained away, gradually graying the landscape to the familiar graphite tones of her childhood. Ashton grasped her hand as she cried, and in the next months led her through the dimming surroundings, reviewing her future world by touch. One night in November Ashton turned out the pale light above their bed, and Lucia awoke to her lasting night the next morning.

DYSFUNCTIONAL

GENTLEMAN AT PLAY

The letter from Aggie, four years after I had seen her last, came as a surprise. She'd come to Boston in 1997 to see me after Helen died, but seemed less outgoing than on her previous visits to us, after the death of Aggie's son Colin. After 1997, she and Bryce might as well have ceased to exist. All I had since were impersonal, breezy notes on Christmas cards preprinted with their names.

"Jared," she began, "I wonder whether you could come for a visit sometime next month. I don't get to Boston much. The farm is a lovely place to relax, and with your schedule, you should be able to spare a few days to renew old ties. We'd love to have you. Give me a call. Hope you are well. Affectionately, Aggie." When I phoned to arrange the visit, Bryce answered with a hearty greeting and handed me directly over to Aggie.

"Oh, Jar,"she said, "it will be wonderful to see you. I can't chat now, but we'll have plenty of time when you're here. How's mid-August?" Her subdued tone—thankful, almost relieved—reminded me of how she spoke as she fell into Helen's arms at the Back Bay station after Colin died. The visit would be my first to the farm after they had exiled themselves from Boston years before. Then fifty, Bryce, in one of his bold moves, retired from Metrix Medicom—with a 24K golden parachute and obscene stock options—to become what he called a 'gentleman at play.' My laptop (a Metrix, in fact) could keep me company when they were busy with other things. As a freelancer, I even thought there might be a *Green Acres* story in the visit, assuming they were as content as their Currier and Ives Christmas cards tried to imply.

The Amtrak slid out from Back Bay station just after noon on a new railbed, past Route 128 and through the towns and woods of central Massachusetts. Modern as the car was, the rhythm and views of the small towns and forest reminded me of my trips to camp in upstate New York as a child. The clear skies evoked memories of the old click of rails, the rattle of the prewar cars, the look of the wires dipping and rising from pole to pole, and the green, green countryside in early summer when the blooming clouds filled the blue sky like my inflated hopes of the month to come.

Bryce's image had become indistinct in my mind, like old, grainy newspaper photos in the *Herald.* Smart, solid, and quick as a quarterback, he had left a trail of friends, admirers, and enemies behind when he and Aggie bought the farm in western Massachusetts to conquer the hard landscape of her forbears. Its main crop at first was frost-heaved rocks like those that farmers from Puritan times used to enclose their modest properties.

After three and a half hours, the train pulled into Pittsfield, where I stepped out into the warm afternoon. I expected to see a gentleman in L. L. Bean chinos and heavy boots. Ten people or so got off with me, whisked away by their mates after a kiss and a hug. I finally caught sight of Bryce with his shock of white hair, black eyebrows and quizzical smile leaning against the interior corner of the shelter on the platform, apparently waiting for me to recognize him. Dressed comfortably in a dress shirt, a light brown vest and no tie, he made eye contact and strode over to me, almost as though I'd been gone just for the day. His handshake was firm, and a ready smile came to his face. Age had left him creased, but alert. His hands were uncalloused, but the tip of his right index finger was missing, a sign that he might do a few farm chores, if not well. In fact, as he explained later, it was a sign of his beginning carpentry in his barn, an explanation that at the time seemed perfectly plausible to me.

"Wonderful to see you, Jared." His courtly voice and shining eyes had lost none of their appeal. He was still a businessman. "Aggie's been looking forward to seeing you." His eyes narrowed, sizing me up.

"Well, I am delighted to get to see you in your new haunts. I can't wait to see the estate. You look pretty well preserved."

He picked up my bag and swept his other hand toward the parking lot. "Hope you've had a good trip. Train was right on time." He led me down the platform with a rolling, stiff-backed walk. We stopped at a muddy Mercedes of recent vintage, which he beeped with his remote to open the trunk. "Sorry to greet you with this. It's Aggie's, but it was blocking the garage door." He slung my bag into the trunk and motioned me around to the passenger side.

He negotiated his way out of the town toward the main road south. I had always thought Bryce and Aggie, about ten years his junior, were oddly matched, a New York entrepreneur transplanted to Route 128 and a scholarship girl, daughter of a middle-class dairy farmer. Helen had met her at Radcliffe in 1971, where they became confidantes and finally roommates in their last year. Helen knew even then that Aggie would build a good life for herself. And so it was. She joined Bryce's firm in 1978, and long before their marriage almost a decade later, she became Bryce's partner, the vice president and canny guide to the business tar-pits that might otherwise have mired him.

After their marriage, she took a stronger public role, radiating confidence at business and social affairs, to which she wore simple, stylish dresses and little jewelry. She had picked up a continental charm by close study of old-money Brahmins, and earlier, I was sure, Helen's social graces. She and Bryce genuinely enjoyed the Boston Symphony and the Museum, to which they made substantial donations. With many connections solidified by Aggie, they swam as important fish in the city's social pond, even after Aggie had Colin in 1989. In fact, Helen told me that Aggie wanted a child before it was too late, and that had precipitated hers and Bryce's marriage. Colin was born in Boston, and, as best as Helen and I could tell, it was Bryce who decided to retire two years later at fifty and abruptly moved them out to the farm.

I was still curious that this marriage had survived. Behind this was the sense, when I knew them before, that it was a mutually faithful, respectful, but somewhat business-like union that endured on obscure understandings in the darkness of their hearts about success. Their most serious shock came when Colin died in a fall at the farm. Aggie was beside herself with the loss. She often came to Boston to seek solace with old friends. Helen and I put her up during these visits, and the old casual, forthright, younger Aggie seemed to assert herself as Helen and she went long into the night talking of the good, bad and ugly times since college. When Helen died, Aggie still came, this time to comfort me, but she stayed with other friends. Aggie was my best connection to Helen, and I loved her for her concern.

Bryce broke my reverie. "So how is your work, Jared?" He had brought the car to a cruising speed that verged on the dangerous once we were on the main road south.

"It's okay. I'm working on a donor crisis at the BSO, just wrapping up the piece for the *Globe*. You may have heard about it. Subscriptions aren't carrying the costs, never have. They're making lots of appeals now, and you've probably gotten their mailings."

"Left that all behind, Jar. Gave enough in the past." The forest canopy of oak and black walnut made a tunnel for the road, patches of second-growth trees and undergrowth too dense to see into even in the bright late afternoon. In the dry summer, the weeds at the side of the road had browned, and dust rose behind us. "Lots of projects out here. Had to clear the land, build outbuildings, revamp the barn. With a lot of paid help, of course, but it's looking good now."

"What do you do for fun? It's a long way from Boston." I thought of Aggie, elbows on our kitchen table years before, too sad to go to shows or exhibits, just talking and drinking moderate Jack Daniels with us in our Somerville apartment. And Colin wasn't the only thing she was sad about. I knew she didn't feel at home at the farm, forbears or no forbears.

"Gotten into politics. The little townships need to share police, ambulance service, fire protection, water, stuff like that. Just need to get these craggy New Englanders off their duff. They need to leave the 19th century behind, skip the 20th, and wake up to the 21st. Had Medicom donate computers to every town hall and library. I'm getting a handle on their problems."

"Leave you any time to harvest your beans and chard?"

"Not much of that. Mainly apples, pumpkins, some pigs. You'll see. Aggie got the horses. Good place to ride, takes her back to when she was a kid. You didn't think I came here to farm did you?" He smiled like he'd just made a deal. We came out into the open. The sun stood in the south, baking the hilly land and blinding me. Farms, fenced in crossed timbers or stone walls, rushed by. "Fact, I'm thinking of clearing a landing strip."

I didn't feel like asking about Aggie. I'd see her soon enough.

* * *

We reached the farm in the late golden afternoon. The sun had begun to dip early behind a large hill to the southwest, silhouetting a wooden tower topped by a small cabin, like a look-out. Nearer the road, an orchard extended to the right and grassy lawns surrounded the house. The barn at the left had a white fenced area, a corral for the two sleek horses. A farm hand was lunging one of them around a well trodden dirt circle at one end. The entire spread was far larger than I had imagined, but without pictures or previous visits, I should not have had any expectations. The graveled driveway behind the house split into several dirt roads, one up the hill and the other leading around the orchard. The car came crunching to a stop at the garage door. We got out of the car into a hot, gnat-filled atmosphere, almost oppressive even for August. A peaceful scene, though, especially if Bryce and Aggie could use it as a backdrop for whatever else they did.

"Here we are. Plenty of room to roam." Bryce squinted against the sun. "Let's get on in. Aggie's waiting."

Aggie opened the door as we approached it. Even through the screen door, I saw an older Aggie than I had expected, her face betraying a trace of the sadness we'd shared in the past. I shuffled in, and her old, winning smile broke through as I put my bag down and gave her a long hug. "Aggie, its marvelous to see you."

"Thanks so much for coming, Jar. It's lovely to see you again too." We detached and I looked at her more closely. She was handsome in a New England way, a bit bonier now, with gray-streaked hair she made no attempt to dye. Her lower jaw, thrust slightly forward, gave her an air of authority that had made her stand out in business and social circles. "Bry," she said, turning to him, "show Jar to the guest room. "Thanks so much. Jar, freshen up and come down right away, and we can have a drink and revisit our youth." I followed Bryce up the stairs to a finely furnished bedroom with elegant faux-rustic furniture, pictures of horses and rural scenes, lace curtains and a private bath. A small TV stood incongruously on a low table by the dresser.

When I came down, Aggie met me at the foot of the stairs. Her deep eyes and white-streaked hair rendered her a model of Boston society, the sort with charities and evening events at the heart of her life. She led me into the living room, a long paneled space with a view toward the barn and a décor resembling that of my guest suite. Bryce sat at one end with a newspaper and rose to greet me. "Well, Bryce, you've certainly made a great thing of this farm house. I'm sorry I haven't seen it till now. I could have pictured you here more properly. Very nice." I hoped this was not a reproach for never having returned Helen's and my invitations.

"We like it," Aggie said. "It was work, but we're comfortable. What'll you have?"

"Scotch? Straight up."

"Bry, could you get the drinks? I'll have the same. And there's some cheese and nuts on the counter." With a smile and a slight nod, he turned and left for the kitchen. She turned to me, serious, looking at me as though she were delivering a warning. "Jar, I really am glad you came. We have to talk. Later. We'll find time." What was that all about? It was hard to smile. Aggie saw the question in my face and raised her hand to preclude my voicing it.

"Okay." My heart stepped up its pace as I assumed my new role, whatever it was. "Anyway, it's great to be here."

A crash of breaking glass came from the kitchen. Aggie started and turned her head to the door. "Bry, what is it?"

"Nothing. We have another bottle. Come get the drinks while I clean this up." I could smell liquor, easily. Aggie went out and returned with our drinks, then back for the hors d'oeuvres. Some mumbled talk reached me amidst the sound of glass being gathered.

Aggie returned, her square face troubled but lit with an amused smile and a shake of the head. "Bry is a bit clumsy now and then. I should have done it myself. But now tell me about yourself, Jar. It's been years, maybe three or four since I visited you. I still see your stories in the paper. I hope you're enjoying it as much as you did before."

Before, yes, before. Before Helen died. I told her about my increasing journalistic responsibilities and commissions in the art and entertainment world, the features, the interviews, the book on Georg Solti I was working on, which never advanced beyond the public face everyone already knew. Eventually, Bryce returned with his own drink, apologizing for the interruption, as he called it. We settled into a conversation of reminiscences about our early days, about the time Helen and Aggie roomed together, their parting paths after graduation, and how she and Bryce got together. I was surprised to learn that she and Bryce, almost immediately after Aggie had been hired at Metrix, had become 'intimate'—didn't Helen tell you?—and had enjoyed continuing success thereafter. Bryce expanded on his most daring exploits, buying up medical equipment companies and designing software and eventually the diagnostic hardware itself as computers became essential elements of the trade. Aggie looked uncomfortable during this conversation, and I got a hint of something yet to come. It was all about her diverting Bryce from sticky situations that sounded as though they might border on the illegal, although when the story got to this point, Bryce abruptly changed the subject.

What the hell was I doing out here? The conversation, through dinner and early evening, never verged on the intimate again, once the topic of the business was dropped. Not once did their child Colin come up, to my increasing relief. But to my increasing dismay, the mystery of Aggie's need to talk privately remained hanging in the air we all breathed, as though she might not find a way of dispelling it. It continued the next day at breakfast, which Aggie served in style and very much to my liking—eggs and sausage and English muffin. And a superior brew of coffee. The morning was as bright as the day before, and as the sun warmed the air, the birds became rare and the cicadas began their concert. From the dining room windows, I could see one farm hand at the barn and another near by raking the gravel of the driveway. I could also see two others caring for the horses and—to my surprise—a sow with piglets emerging from the barn into a sty at one side. The gentleman at play was well cared for.

"Let me show you around today, Jar," Bryce said as I put down my final cup of coffee. "There's lots you can't see from here. Aggie's got to deal with bills and the horses, so that leaves us free to explore."

"Sounds fine." I felt this would be a good beginning, even if *Green Acres* was not in the cards. Aggie smiled, agreeing with Bryce, and rose to clear the table.

I had not noticed the dented headlight frame on Aggie's car the day before, which left the unit somewhat askew. After the drive with Bryce yesterday I wondered how often he borrowed her car and whether the damage was his. We piled in and he backed and turned onto the lane out beyond the house. We stopped a short distance later at the barn. It was newly restored after they arrived, Bryce told me, from a graying wreck with a barely legible ad on its side to a solid structure with red clapboard siding and a clean interior. I got out and looked inside. There was hay in the loft and stalls for the horses and an inner pen for the sow and her babies. The smells filled me with memories of camp. Hay, manure, the summer delight of my blighted life.

Bryce hadn't left the car. "I should have rebuilt this from scratch," he said, after I got back in. "I didn't know Aggie would want horses until later."

"I hope Aggie didn't find it too much of an adjustment. She seemed to love the social life in Boston."

"She's okay. At least she has me to organize, and she's beginning to enjoy it. It was actually easier at first, though, you know, with the kid." He looked away and turned to the car. The kid. Time to move on, both of us. It struck me there were no children's outdoor things around house or barn, no rusted swing or some little child's hut or a bicycle. Erased, no memories.

"So what's that tower up there?" I pointed to the hill with its little shed on stilts.

"That's the observatory. A good place for it, especially out here with so little light pollution. Don't use it now. Let me show you the woods, trails. I like to get away from the house now and then. Very relaxing." I got back in the car and Bryce backed and raced up the road around the apple orchard toward the woods, bouncing out of ruts and potholes like he was on an all-terrain race. I found myself holding on to the seat, glad I was wearing a seat-belt, unlike Bryce. For the first time, I could see the extensive barbed-wired field, probably for the horses far to our left. We went on and parked at the wood's edge next to a grand oak. We got out and Bryce led me into the cool forest. Dead bundles of underbrush lay about at its edge.

"Took a while to clear the field this far back. The guys spent a year with tractors and dozers pulling out stumps, rocks, everything. I can't see how the farmers of the 17th century cleared this land. I'm clearing the underbrush now back into the woods, what's left of them." He looked into the forest proudly, with his hands hooked into the back pockets of his pants. We walked into the open area for a few hundred feet. I was impressed by what he had accomplished and said so. But it was not a lot of fun looking into a deep forest, and there wasn't much of a trail to take us farther in.

"Do you think we could go up to observatory? Love to see it, I loved astronomy as a kid. Can hardly remember the constellations now. I deal with other kinds of stars." Bryce smiled at my attempt at humor, the very first of the day.

"If you like. Haven't been up for a while, but I don't think there's much to see." We drove back toward the house and took the other fork up the hill. The dirt road was overgrown, but passable. Bryce took it as though it was paved, heedless of hidden irregularities in the road. After less than a mile, we were at the crest near the tower and stopped. I felt I could breathe again. The tower, over fifteen feet tall, was unattended and showed signs of weathering and a lack of upkeep. Standing beside it, I could see out over a forest that continued for miles around, with two or three small townships, each with a steeple or two, in the distance. This was New England at its best. At least if you like to look at pictures. The heat was more intense in this open spot and I wished I had brought a hat.

"You mind if I climb up and see the view from up there? You have a telescope?"

"Not much to see. Telescope was stolen years ago. And I didn't bring binocs. Sorry about that. Didn't expect to need 'em. Fact, I'm not sure it's really that safe."

Four beams, set in a concrete platform, tapered inward toward the top, with crossed timbers holding them in position. The structure was still strong, so I swung onto the rungs leading upward. Bryce watched, squinting against the sun. "Be careful, Jar," was all he said. I reached the cabin. The little entrance did not have a door, and I decided I'd best not try to enter. Looking into the interior, about six feet square, I saw a tripod near an opening that must have been a telescope mount. Another structure in the center might have been another mount for a reflector. The roof was arranged in panels, hinged to be opened downward for vertical observations. One of them had fallen and lay on the floor. There was little else to see in the cabin except some very old snack wrappings, a small wool cap and a red rubber ball.

* * *

I stepped back down the laddered side of the tower, feeling the danger of the height this time, as I had to look down. Bryce leaned against the car in the pose I had first seen him on the Pittsfield train platform.

I was unnerved by my visit up the tower and searched for some obvious, neutral questions as we got back into the car. Instead I blurted out "I have to say I'm sorry about your son." The red ball in the observatory must have triggered that and for a moment my breath went short as I envisioned little Colin, all of five, clattering down the rungs of the ladder to his death. We knew he died in a fall, but not the circumstances. I continued awkwardly, "Helen and I were shocked, and we know it hit Aggie pretty hard. I hope she's recovered by now, but I'm glad Helen could be there when Aggie needed her."

"Well, I am too. Don't tell her I told you, but it's put us a bit apart. When it comes up, Aggie gets on me about it, sounding like my goddamn mother." He lurched the car back onto the road, having swept into the brush. He became silent, more attentive to where he was going.

I was glad to get back to the house to take a rest in my pleasant guest room. How many gentlemen farmers complain about their goddamn mothers? I felt like a stranger. How many captains of industry, I asked myself, go to live on a farm to play politics in the backwaters of Massachusetts? Somehow the life course of Aggie and Bryce didn't quite compute.

I was relieved when at dinner they laid out plans for a tour of the region, a visit to a cider mill, and seeing some of the more picturesque towns in the area. And I finally recognized one of my main roles here: to insert myself into their silence and tell them what was happening in the Hub. They referred to occasional visits from Aggie's friends from Boston, but I was better connected and could bring them up to date on politics and society since they had left.

During the next two days, we went to a James Levine concert in Tanglewood nearby at my request. I was happy to learn that they contributed after all to this wonderful organization, continuing their allegiance to the BSO. The day after, we had seen the Rockwell museum in Stockbridge and the nearby Shaker communities. These tours were more than I had expected, with the weather obliging by becoming cooler. We now became better acquainted again, more relaxed with each other.

Three days after I arrived, Bryce had to go for a day back to Pittsfield, the Berkshire county seat, for business. When Bryce told us of this, I was briefly tempted to go with him to get the train back before the spell of amity broke. But I could not ignore the obligation of talking to Aggie, of resolving the nagging question of what the hell she had to say.

Bryce left after our late breakfast, saying he would return for dinner. I helped Aggie clear the table and do the dishes. The kitchen clashed with the décor of the remainder of the house, being state of the art stainless throughout, with all the conveniences Aggie might need. She was proud of her cooking, and rightly so, having served us plain, elegant breakfasts, game hen and wild rice and zucchini one night and an incomparable rack of lamb the next. All of this somewhat understated, in keeping with the modest style and lack of excess I associated with this part of New England. But the fully equipped kitchen and Aggie's sheer efficiency made up for the lack of a hired cook. She considered it, she said, her favorite domain out here, with the horses coming in second. In fact, she was writing a cookbook—a clumsily titled *Menus from Mass*—with Bryce a willing critic of the experimental dishes, for which he supplied well-chosen wines. This seemed to be their remaining joint project, and I was happy to be its beneficiary.

From the kitchen we retired to the living room, and the morning sun highlighted strands of Aggie's graying hair as she sat on the sofa, her hand on the cushion and hesitant look seeming to invite me to sit down beside her. I took a stuffed chair facing her.

"Aggie," I said, thinking it would be easier if I opened, "you said you had something to talk about. I've been wondering ever since what it might be." I am not a journalist for nothing. I'd had a number of difficult questions to put to people now and again.

"Jar, thanks for asking. I don't know where to begin. I just want to talk, that's all. How are you enjoying yourself?"

"Here, or in my exalted career?"

"Well, here in general. Would you like another cup of coffee? I forgot to ask in the kitchen."

"No more for me, thanks, Aggie. I came here to relax. And I am enjoying being here. I didn't realize you had so much to see so near. The concert was wonderful." Aggie was not good at small talk, and the talk was getting pretty small. "So I should ask you the same thing. How are you enjoying yourself? Bryce seems to have found his way."

"He has, Jar, and I'm afraid I've lost mine. It's been such a complicated life, and I never thought it would end up this way. I'm only fifty-one. I was willing to come out here and that all changed when, you know, Colin…was taken from us. I just wish Helen were here, for both of us."

The image of the red rubber ball seized me. I could not help myself. "Aggie, how did Colin die? I mean where and everything?" My breath came short as I waited.

"It was in the barn. We had some cows then. Colin was an adventurous little fellow. He'd taken to jumping into the hay from the beam along the loft. He loved the thrill and we tried to discourage it, but it happened. There just wasn't enough hay there to cushion him that day. I don't want to think about it. Bry brought him back down in the car and we called an ambulance. But of course it takes forever for them to get here this far from town."

"I'm so sorry, Aggie. I admire your strength in picking yourself up. Helen did too."

"She was a big help." Aggie's eyes glistened. "The worst was that Bry and I had a huge argument the day before about that very thing. Colin loved the observatory and I dreaded the time Colin might try to climb up there by himself if Bry wasn't there to watch. But Bry refused to get organized and take the rungs off it, or just tear it down." Her face twisted and her mouth turned down, on the verge of a sob. "No need now." Then she cried as though her lifeless child had just been brought into the room. I had no idea she was capable of such outward pain. Her shoulders shook like she had a violent cough.

"Aggie! For heaven's sake! I'm so sorry, how can I help?" I could not believe the violence of her grief, seven years old.

Aggie regained her composure in several steps. She seemed about to speak, then would quietly cry again, getting up to get tissues from the escritoire near the window. "Jared, this won't let me go. I'm sorry. I just needed to talk."

"It's a long time ago, Aggie. You seemed to be doing all right. Is there…anything else?"

With a final snuffle, she wiped her eyes. "Oh, there's everything else, Jar." She waved her hand vaguely.

"I think I'd like some coffee." I got up. "I can get it myself. Will you have some?"

Aggie nodded to say she would, plainly welcoming the break.

I brought the coffee out. Aggie now stood at the window looking out at the hill behind the barn. She returned to the sofa as I put the coffee down on the coffee table between us. "So, Aggie, again, I'm so sorry about all this. Tell me whatever else there is, if you'd like. I'm a good listener. As a journalist, I should say 'Off the record.'"

"Off the record." Aggie took a sip of coffee. She became the businesswoman again, talking coherently and objectively about things. She said she had not told anyone about the way she and Bryce had succeeded, and why they were still together.

Some of Bryce's moves, it appears, were dangerous, and Aggie became vague in describing them, as though she could not be completely open even with me. A major acquisition, it seemed, brought with it a patent on a modified software design enabling fast parallel processing in a simple computer. When they discovered that Microsoft had developed essentially the same thing, Bryce mounted a major campaign for Metrix to sue.

"The board agreed, and it was a heady time for all of us. Suffice it to say," Aggie went on, "we had to revisit the old acquisition paperwork and our patent drafts. I found disturbing irregularities in the acquisition and became terrified of a major scandal. I began to push Bryce hard to get Metrix to drop the whole thing. Fortunately Microsoft couldn't seem to find their case either with all the complexities of the business, and so the thing was dropped for the time being. But Microsoft could reopen the case at a later time, if they wanted."

"But it sounds as though it all turned out okay, then."

"Yes, in some respects. But inevitably the board revisited the acquisition and our counsel urged the company to relieve us of interests except for the options. We were bought off."

"Off the record, does this mean you're living under some sort of threat?"

"Possibly, but only if the suit gets revised by someone at Metrix unaware of the risks produced by Bryce's faulty management and poor judgment in pressing the Microsoft suit. Needless to say, Bryce and I argued endlessly about how to proceed, and in the end it was only his suggestion that we come out here and lead a wholly new life that gave us the truce we needed to continue."

"Quite a story, Aggie. I don't know what to say, and won't say anything."

"Thanks. You're a good man, Jar. I haven't told anyone about this and it's a relief to tell you today."

The afternoon had grown long, and we'd hardly moved. It was about three thirty, and the poignant grief of the morning had been replaced by the squalor of business misdeeds and marital conflicts. I didn't feel like asking directly why she remained with Bryce.

"Aggie, are you obliged to live this one out? Any thoughts of you guys moving back to Boston?"

"Bry's having fun for a change, and he's determined to hang onto me. We decided without really deciding that we'll carry this burden together. It would be a lot heavier for either of us if we were alone, and even worse if we were with anyone else. We have at least one conscience between us. I hope you can forget all this Jar, but it's just such a relief to talk."

"We've shared some miseries, Aggie, but I had no idea you were living with this. Especially difficult after losing Colin too."

Aggie began to shake again. "Colin shouldn't have been allowed into the loft or into the observatory. And if we didn't live in the middle of nowhere because of his father, he could have been saved."

She turned away and leaned on the armrest, her forehead in her hand, covering her eyes. I regretted mentioning Colin, the more so as she again broke down completely, sobbing quietly into a handkerchief she brought to her face. I got up and sat beside her and put my hand on her back. She turned and put both her arms around me and wept on my shoulder, bubbling and holding me as though she were drowning in her own tears. I was the first to hear the car come up the short driveway, and the tires crunch on the gravel as the car came to a fast stop.

The car door slammed as Aggie drew away, but before I could stand up, Bryce was in the door, yelling about "those geriatric pricks in North Adams!" It was all he said before he saw us.

"Now what the fuck is going on? What are you guys up to?" He stood still, his legs apart, holding a roll of papers. His eyes were slits as he looked at us.

"Don't get excited, Bry. We were talking about Colin. I got emotional." Aggie had recovered rapidly, but dabbed conspicuously at her eyes. "I haven't had anyone to talk to, Bry. I'm sorry. It's nothing."

I hoped the tears would convince him that we were not about to go to bed. But what does he know about Aggie and her visits to me after Helen died? I was tongue-tied, murmuring apologies that Aggie was really upset and that I hoped Bryce could calm her and give her the support she needed. At least one of us standing about there was superfluous, and I felt if there were anything Bryce wanted to tell me, it could wait till he and Aggie had it out. I excused myself, again mumbling that I felt they should be alone.

In the guest bedroom, I could hear soft voices from downstairs. The farmhouse was not so lightly built that I could hear what was being said, but things were being said quietly, rationally. No wailing from Aggie, no angry words from Bryce. I did not dare open my door a crack, but Aggie was doing most of the talking, speaking in the voice in which she told me her business story. I wished that I could get the internet on the laptop, but there was no dial-up or Ethernet opportunity in the guest room, even if Bryce was a mover and shaker in the industry. The TV offered news at the end of the afternoon, and I gave myself over to it and other programs that held no interest for me. For some reason, I did not want to try to reconstruct the conversation with Aggie to see what I could make of the hints of illegality in the business story. It would almost be like telling it to someone else, and instinctively I wanted to forget the whole thing.

"Jared." Bryce's voice at the door. I had not heard him ascend the carpeted stairs. It was about six o'clock. I opened the door. He looked chastened, contained, the businessman with something to discuss. "Sorry about all that, Jar. Aggie's not herself now and again, especially when it comes to, you know, the boy. She'll never get over that, and I can only do so much. I'm not very good at what I do."

"I'm sorry too, Bryce. I should be comforting you as well. And I felt Aggie needed some sympathy and I'm sorry how it looked. I was amazed at how her pain has lasted. I didn't expect that."

"Forget about it. She's fixing something to eat. Not your most elegant meal, but it'll get us through the night. Let's go down and have a drink."

"Thanks, Bryce." I followed him down the stairs. The drinks did nothing for either of us, and we sat looking at each other glumly. He volunteered little about his trip to Pittsfield, and I tried to bring him up on the news, which I had largely forgotten. Aggie came in with some olives and cheese, and shortly she brought us to the table. She looked strong again, apologizing for killing the day.

"You know, Aggie and Bryce, I feel I know both of you much better now," I said, looking at them each in turn. "Whatever the difficult time we've all had, I feel we're much closer." I hoped both of them would see this as excusing all of us, and reminding them that we had been good friends and I wouldn't be embarrassed if they weren't embarrassed. "I've had a wonderful time here, and it's so good to be with you again. I loved seeing this part of the state, and I can't imagine that Berkshire County won't be the richer for your efforts, Bryce."

It wasn't the best speech I ever did, but it took some of the tension out. And I went on to say that I would overstay my welcome if I stayed more than another night, and I felt that I should go tomorrow after all. Bryce made no objection, and Aggie betrayed none in her expression. The train would come at nine and I could get it if we all got up early. We got a little more conversational after that, and they wished me well. I finished my wine and excused myself, and went on upstairs.

I could not sleep. The moon was bright and I looked at the ceiling as I began slowly to reconstruct, after all, the story behind the marriage, the feelings behind the faces, the legal contortions behind the business. The grandfather clock in the upstairs hall struck midnight, then one o'clock.

A flicker of light trembled on the ceiling, growing brighter. I heard urgent sounds from outside, becoming louder. I went to the window. The barn was burning. The horses bellowed and raged in their stalls. The heat, I thought, the high heat. Bryce and Aggie were nowhere to be seen.

Later it was clear why. Shot dead in their bedroom, with a gun with a silencer. Was it Aggie who set fire to the barn where her son had fallen to his death? Surely, she would never have done that to her beloved horses.

REUNION

"Ben! Is that you?" It was lunch time and Ben was having a sausage and a beer.

Ben looked up from the counter of the upscale diner. He turned and saw a familiar figure waving from a booth by the window. The June sun behind the figure made it hard to recognize the face. But the voice and the tilt of his head told Ben it was Martin despite the years since they had seen one another.

"Ben, over here! Come on over." It was indeed Martin. Ben picked up his plate of sausage and his beer and joined him in the window booth. Martin's shirt was white, his tie neat, his moustache trimmed. His face was lined. Darkness shaded the skin under his dark brown eyes, from overwork or overindulgence. "What're you doing here, Ben?"

"Better yet, what're you doing here? I haven't seen you since the tenth college reunion."

Martin took a sip of his wine and put the glass down. "Just came back. The bank was good to me, transferred me back to Missouri as a manager. It's not Santa Fe, but there's more money to be made in a suburb like Clayton than in many big cities. I live in Clayton too. And until today I figured I could take the humidity." Martin loosened his tie a little.

"So how's Carol taking it?"

"We're divorced. Long story. But it finally looks like Tam and I can get together after all. One of the reasons I came back."

"Tamara! I thought that was over when you left Washington U."

"It was. As you know, she went and married money. Old French money from down by the river. But as they say, the flame burns on if nobody blows it out. She says Hubby's getting sick of her independent ways. She wants out real bad, and he's willing to pay if she leaves quietly, behaves herself. There's a reputation at stake. His."

"Jesus, Martin, that's a hell of a long time to wait."

Martin lowered his voice. "Don't tell anyone, Ben, but it hasn't been uninterrupted."

"I get it. When's she gonna be free?"

"Sometime soon. I'll let you know. What brings you to St. Louis?"

Ben took a bite of sausage and a sip of beer. "Moved back here five years ago. Like you say, divorce, long story. Megan figured there were livelier men. No kids, so she left. I came back mainly to take care of Mother. I live near her in a little house off Big Bend."

"You seeing anyone?"

"Not really."

"Look, I've gotta go, but let's get together and catch up. I've got to get back to work now, but I want to talk some more.

"Great idea. Today's not a good day, but the end of the week is fine. You know Grant's down in the Loop?"

"Is it still there? Sure. It'll be great to be back in Grant's." As Martin sidled to the end of the booth, they agreed to meet there on Friday at 5:30.

"5:30 it is. Great to see you."

Ben looked up as Martin rose and took his suit jacket from the hook on the post at the end of the booth. It's funny, Ben thought, how you can pick up with a pal after ten years like the conversation never stopped. He thought of how Martin married Carol, a shy, moneyed daughter from University City, like she was something good for business. He was an attractive match, active, gregarious, someone to bring Carol out. But, Ben thought, Carol had too few social skills to be married to a businessman. A little too retiring for Martin. Ben often wished he'd met her first.

"Kind of glad now that I didn't. I wonder where she is now?" He brought himself up short and smiled. He didn't realize he was whispering these thoughts, and turned to see if anyone had heard.

* * *

Martin was late, but Ben had taken a small table in a corner of the bar. He sipped a beer and played with the coaster. Anheuser-Busch. Pride of St. Louis, along with the Arch. The Delmar Loop outside Grant's had been tidied up since Ben's and Martin's high school and university days, with the streetcar tracks gone now and the whole place coming back to life after a lot of effort over the years.

Martin, the gray suited banker, with his head held high and smiling down on the crowd, threaded his way to Ben's tiny table. "So, old friend, tell me about yourself," he said, after he sat down. "It's so great to see you!" He motioned to the waitress, who took his martini order. Ben asked for another beer.

"Not a whole hell of a lot to report. Mother's doing well in assisted living, and I'm getting on just fine. When I moved back from Minnesota after working at Sears, I figured I'd see if I could get into Macy's. Didn't have to look far. Got a managerial job in men's clothing first thing and here I am."

"After five years or whatever, you must be lonely. What do you do with yourself?"

"Friends from work. Sports. Theater. Symphony."

"Sounds pretty dull. Like U City in the old days. That's why I left. Do you see anyone from back then? Must be a bunch of them still here." Martin put his glass to his lips and looked over it to Ben.

"Yeah, but they've all got families and we've all really grown apart," Ben said with a palms-up shrug. This is going to be a tough get-together, he thought. Men's department talking to a bank. But there was a lot he couldn't say. Martin was always more interesting.

"C'mon, Ben, you can't just sit here and tell me you do nothing every night and weekend. You were pretty quiet back then, but you found a pretty good life with a pretty good chick. What happened?"

"Nothing. That's how Megan put it, and she meant it— nothing. I'm just a dull, loving guy. She might have been happy with kids, but she couldn't conceive and I wasn't going to make special efforts. When she didn't either, I kind of knew our time was up." Ben looked away toward the bar. The mirror reflected the folks at the counter, anonymous in the low light, ignored by the bartender. "No hard feelings. Soon enough she found someone that juiced her up. We're in touch now and again."

"So you sit around waiting for Sleeping Beauty to appear? You gotta go wake her up first."

Ben hesitated for a moment. Then he lowered his voice and said, "To tell the truth, Martin, if you'll keep it to yourself, I'm in a good place. I met someone young. Too young, probably, like twenty-two, just out of college." He smiled. "You might want to call me a lecher, but she says I'm the best of the breed."

"Well," Martin said, "now we're getting somewhere. What's she like? What's her name?"

"I call her Dawn. She likes that. Solid. Grounded. Mature, thank god. She's had to field a lot of drama with her mother, and finally had to leave home. She won't tell me anything about her family or them about me because of our ages. I haven't introduced her to my mother either. Met her a year and a half ago at Christmas. She worked as a temp in the store. Now she's independent, with money from a trust when she turned twenty-one. She's in graduate school now. Moved in with me till she gets oriented about things."

"You think this is for real?"

"You never know, Martin. I'm crazy about her. We stay below everyone's radar. Don't go out much except for an occasional get-away. We've talked. You know, even marriage. But that's up to her."

"I hope it works, Ben. These things can be tricky, but when they work, you can go to heaven. I wish I'd started that way with Tam. Good luck."

"Thanks." Ben groped for words, looking away at the other tables, the men and women easing out of the workday before they had to meet the hazards of home. A watering hole whose music and muffled talk from all directions made conversation less urgent. "I hope the best for you too, Martin. Do you and Tam see one another much, or are you just waiting like a buzzard?"

Martin looked narrowly at Ben. "We meet out of town when the coast is clear. I feel like a fucking teenager skulking around in her back yard at night." He fingered the olive from beneath the ice in his glass. "Tell you what: why don't we get together sometime when Big Daddy's away? We have to be careful until the divorce. Some quiet hotel on a weekend when no one's looking. I'm looking for some company and a tiny bit of social life."

"It could be done as far as I'm concerned," Ben said. "We could use some company ourselves. Deal."

That decided, Ben and Martin began to remember old times, old friends, and old hopes, a conversation that took them into a long dinner of bar food and more drinks. Ben felt like he was checking off all the old successes and sadnesses, putting them behind him. Looking at life in the rear-view mirror, he almost felt guilty for the comfort of his new life, his new love. He had given Dawn her affectionate name to celebrate the bright prospects before them every day. Perhaps Martin felt the same, Ben thought, renewed with love for Tam, once lost to him, now at hand. Tam and Martin were an ardent, active item in college, and everyone pitied Martin when she abandoned mere promise for an old man with real wealth.

They parted with pats on the back, and Ben drove home to Dawn for the night.

* * *

They had decided to meet at the Cheshire Hotel in Clayton. Tam would take a room there. The place was frequented neither by bankers nor by the friends of millionaires. Good for privacy.

Ben parked in the lot in front and went into the lobby. It was almost six o'clock. The summer sun was lowering in the west, flooding the lobby with light. He had waited for Dawn at home, but she phoned to say she would be late. A project was keeping her at the lab where she worked. She might be as much as thirty or forty minutes late. "Don't worry, hon," she said. "I'll be there. The experiment's working, but I've got to stay with it."

Ben looked in at the bar. The Fox and Hound was not too crowded, and he could not spot Martin. At the desk, the clerk gave him a message to call Tam's room. She answered. "Ben! It's been such a long time. We'll be right down. Give us a few minutes. We'll meet you in the bar."

"Don't hurry. Dawn'll be coming a little later herself."

Ben returned to the lobby and took a seat with a view of the elevators. Before five minutes had passed, the tall, auburn-haired Tamara, clothed in a sweeping dark-blue dress emerged, Martin behind her. Ben stood, impressed by the suavity of her movements and poise. She had been awkward in college, but he suspected she had practiced her manner for some time, moving as she did in the rich climate of St. Louis society. Martin was as natty as ever, looking proud of the woman in front of him. Tam came to Ben and threw her arms around him, air-kissing him on both cheeks. "Oh Ben, it's like we're young again. I'm so glad Martin found you and suggested this."

"I'm sorry Dawn won't be here for a bit," Ben said.

"Let's get a drink while we're waiting." Tam, handsome and commanding, touched both men on the shoulder. Martin took her arm and strode, Ben behind them, into the bar, where in the dusk of low lights and dark paneling, they found a table and four seats. Ben positioned himself to watch for Dawn in the lobby.

"Ben, Martin told me about Dawn and how you met a while ago." She turned to Martin. "A mart, the usual." Martin signaled the waitress, and ordered two martinis and a beer for Ben. "What's been happening," Tam continued, "since 1980?"

"Not a lot, Tam. It's been pretty steady except for a few bumps along the way. Martin told you about Megan? Not too painful a break, but it left me a little drifting. But I've done pretty well, and we parted friends. Sort of."

"'Sort of' is the watchword in divorces," Martin said, "like 'sort of expensive' or 'sort of devastating.'" He pulled his chair nearer the table as the drinks came, Tam's straight up and Martin's on the rocks. "Nothing is easy. But it sounds like you were luckier than I was. Or Tam is."

Tam looked up as she raised her glass. "Here's to the future. All of us." She sipped a polite sip and then a longer one. She gave Martin a grin. "I am so ready to be in the open again with someone I adore."

"A few more months, sweets, and we're home free. Then I may not have to work any more," he winked at her.

"Who says I'm going to share the loot?" Tam smiled at Martin and punched his arm with affection.

"Don't worry, I've got a whole bank to rob." Martin took Tam's hand.

She turned to Ben. "Ben, I'm dying to meet The Dawn. She sounds really good for you from what Martin tells me." She turned back to Martin. "Honey, could you order another mart? I'm out."

Soon some of the memories from the lunch weeks ago were revived for Tam's benefit. Ben had another beer, looked at his watch occasionally, and fell into the conversation with increasing enthusiasm. Dawn was later than he expected, but Tam was loosening up, becoming more open and gesturing like an actress. Her gorgeous curled hair took on a liberated look, more like the old days. Her dramatic manner grew as she spoke of her place in the St. Louis firmament, of groups of women friends from college, and their naughty excursions to New York and L.A. And Santa Fe.

"So," Ben said, "you've been married now, what, twenty-three years? Whatever your troubles, that's kind of a record these days. Look at the friends we've been talking about. And look at us."

Tam looked down at the table and paused. "I've been married forever, Ben. It weren't easy, but I hope it'll be worth it. The son of a bitch is sturdy as an oak, and just as much fun to sleep with."

"Gee, I'm sorry Tam. But it looks like it'll be over soon."

"Can't wait, Ben."

Martin moved closer to Tam. "It's going to be fine, Tam."

Tam ignored him. She looked fixedly at Ben again. "I mean, what do you do with someone that ties you down and walks all over you? Most of the time I'm performing in public for the bastard, and that includes his obnoxious French family. I can't wait to dump him."

Ben and Martin looked at one another with slight frowns at Tam's conclusive smoldering, her face contorted in anger. Martin had not yet finished his second martini. "Take it easy, Tam."

"No, I won't take it easy. We're here and no one knows who the fuck we are. It's like being on parole, so let me be. I'm having a good time." Her watery eyes spoke of other things.

"Tam, we're going to eat soon. Dawn oughta be here any minute."

She better be, Ben thought. At least, only two of them— Ben and Dawn—would have to drive home. Tam would only have to get to her room and throw up there if it came to that.

He looked again out of the bar entrance. "There she is, guys! Finally. I'll go get her."

A young woman, dressed in a black velvet pant-suit, looked around the lobby. She had a quiet beauty, with dusky red hair, and narrow, intelligent eyes. Ben stood and left to meet her, silhouetted by the sun. Dawn finally saw him and smiled brightly as they neared one another. They embraced and turned back into the dark bar. As she adjusted to the darkness, she stopped, arrested in mid-surprise.

"Mother!"

"Michelle! What the hell are you doing here?"

Ben held his breath. Martin too held his breath, looking up at Ben, then turned his face down, leaning his head onto his hand, his elbow on the table.

Dawn—Michelle—turned back into the sunlight and to Ben, her face contorted in a combination of wonder and sob. "Is this a joke?" She turned to leave.

"Michelle! Get the hell back here. Where the hell are you going? Get back here and tell me what you think you're doing!"

"Sit down, Tam! We didn't know. I never met Michelle! I didn't know it was her!"

"The hell you didn't! You tell me next time you want a reunion and I'll tell you to fuck off. Let's go."

"Cool it, Tam. Relax. We're going to the room. Steady." Martin helped her stand, his jaw set, his eyes grim. Ben and Michelle backed away into the lobby as he and Tam came out of the bar, blinded by the setting sun.

They swept past Ben and Michelle. As they turned toward the elevators, Tam looked back and said in a low voice, "Michelle, you slut, run away then screw around with used-up Ben. Lots of luck, kid. Same to you, Benjy. She deserves you. Let go of my arm, Martin."

She lurched into the elevator unsteadily.

"Big Boy," Tam said to Martin when the door closed, "Let's sort this out over another drink when we get upstairs. Meanwhile, just call me Sunset."

ABDUCTION

"I'm surprised you're already home. Too hot for you?" Virginia asked.

"Why are you surprised?"

"Because something came up and I tried to reach you. But they said you were out."

"What happened?"

"I don't know. I saw something from my office window when I was at work. Down on the street. I didn't know what to do."

"An auto accident? Something like that?"

"Harry, I feel stupid. I called the police when I couldn't get you."

"Ginnie, what the hell was it?"

"I was on the phone to San Francisco, and looking down, you know, from the fourth floor, and I see a blue van park at the curb. The driver, a woman, gets out, slams her door and walks off. Then right away a black car parks right behind her van and a man gets out after a minute. He goes around his car to the sidewalk and walks to the van and stops and looks in, and just like that he opens the rear door..."

"Ginnie, slow down. Anyone else in the van?"

"Honey, don't interrupt. That's just it. The man opens the back door and pulls out this blond child dressed in a blue dress. What I remember most is her black shoes and little white socks. It was weird."

"I meant were there other people? What happened with the kid?"

"I had to tell San Francisco I'd call back, and then I saw the man carry the girl back to his car, put her in the back seat, and drive off. I didn't know what to do, but I knew it wasn't good."

"Was anyone in the black car when the guy put the kid in there? I mean did you see him give anyone the kid?"

"I couldn't see. I was rattled, Harry. I buzzed Jane and she came in, but by the time I looked back, the black car was gone. That girl was abducted, Harry. That's what we decided. We called the police. It was hard to convince them to come over and they were skeptical. I showed them from the fourth floor how I saw it all, and then we all went down to the street. It was so hot, and they were really impatient. The van was gone and they acted like they didn't believe a word of it."

"I guess Chicago police have seen a lot of false alarms, and they have other business."

"Harry! You sound just like them. Listen to me."

"I meant they didn't have much physically to go on."

"That's what they said. At least they pretended they were taking notes, and said if they heard anything they'd let me know. I wrote our home number on my card and practically had to force it on them. Jerks. I came home early. If you smell anything, it's my first cigarette in a while."

"Take it easy, Ginnie. I've got to unwind myself."

"I've got to talk about this, hon. I'm so up in the air and can't get what happened out of my head."

"Okay. I'll jump into something comfortable and maybe we can forget the news and have a drink. First let me turn the air conditioner on."

* * *

"So anyhow, what do you make of this?"

"What *can* I make of it, Harry? A woman disappears and her child is stolen while I watch. I never saw her come back and drive off. I wonder if she never knew the girl was gone till she was on the road again."

"It might not be what you think, Ginnie."

"What else could it have been?"

"Well, the whole thing could have been arranged, like a transfer of custody for the weekend. It's Friday, after all."

"That's the dumbest thing I ever heard."

"Here's another possibility. What woman in her right mind would leave a small child in a car on a hot day like this. Maybe the guy saw the girl and decided to take her to the police for her own safety."

"That's even dumber, Harry. This thing didn't look like a rescue to me. It looked a guy looking into a van, seeing a child and stealing her."

"Was the kid struggling and kicking with her little black shoes and white socks?"

"Don't be sarcastic. This is serious."

"I am serious, and I know how you must feel. Especially with the scenario you imagine."

"Give me some more wine, Harry. I didn't imagine anything. I saw it. You just don't care."

"I care about you. What did the woman look like? How did she get out of the car and walk off? You said she slammed the door."

"So you slam car doors when you leave. It doesn't have to mean anything."

"But you made a point of it. How did she seem walking away?"

"I didn't make a point of it. I don't know how she walked away. She just left, crossed the street and disappeared."

"What woman would leave a kid in her car like that?"

"How the hell should I know? Stop cross-examining me. I had enough of that with the police."

"I'm just trying to figure out some other explanation to calm you down."

"Don't patronize me, Harry. It's like you were with the whole fertility thing."

"Are we back to that? I'm shutting up right now if you are. We've moved on. Live with it."

"Thanks to you I have to live with it while you're just relieved you don't have to screw around with a family."

"I did everything I could, sperm counts, screwing you on demand like an experimental chimp."

"I didn't enjoy it either."

"I'd rather talk about your poor little kidnapped sweetie. How old was she?"

"Don't change the subject."

"Who changed the subject? First you're whining about a two-minute drama you see from the fourth floor and now it's how I don't care about your not being able to have kids. How old was the little girl? And don't start raining tears like you always do."

"Harry! I'm telling you about a crime and no one gives a shit, especially you! I'm gonna call the police to see if they ever got a report of a missing child."

"Give it a rest, Ginnie. They probably wouldn't tell you if they did."

"Here I see a girl stolen from her mother. I can't even think of anything else. And you come home from an office full of pretty little paralegals and kick back as though it's a normal day."

"For me, it *is* a normal day. Except for the way you're acting."

"Harry, why don't you just call up Peggy and see if she'd like to meet you for a drink. It's not too late to meet her at your watering hole. She's probably there pining for you."

"Don't start that up again, hon. That's over, and you know it."

"How do I know it? She's there in the office every day."

"You want me to get her fired? I'm gonna top off my martini. Don't go away."

"I wish I could, fucker."

"What did you say?"

"I said I wish I could."

"Wish you could what?"

"Go fucking away, Harry."

"Well maybe you should after all this. Dr. Nolan told us to remember that we had that option if things didn't work out."

"I'm tired of working on it. So are you, Harry."

"To hell with you."

"To hell with you too"

"That's it, Ginnie. I'm outta here." Harry was angry.

"Sounds like you made up your mind awhile ago. You were never really working to make things better."

"I did my best. I'm sick of recriminations. It's never forgive, never forget."

"I could forgive you if you could forgive me. The only reason I got mixed up with James was to see if…" Virginia hesitated.

Harry broke in, "Yeah, to see if someone with herkier, jerkier dancing sperm could do the trick for you. You think that would work in the end?" Harry glowered.

"Harry! Stop it!"

"I'm outta here. That scenario, that fantasy you had—that was you and me and our missing off-spring, wasn't it?

"Fuck you, Harry. Let me open the door for you."

"No need. And if it's any comfort to you, Peggy's pregnant."

MEMOIR

"Hi Dr. Helmsford."

"Lola! What are you doing here at this hour?"

"Sorry to bother you at home, but I just thought I'd bring by a document you might be interested in. It arrived this afternoon and is from one of the patients we've both been caring for recently. It appears to be confidential, and that's why I felt I should deliver it personally. Miss Martin has since died, you'll be sorry to know. But that, and the confidentiality of the message, made me think I should bring this to you in person."

She handed him a square manila envelope. "See," she said. "It's marked 'Strictly Confidential'."

"I'm sorry to hear of her death," said Dr. Helmsford. "It's been several weeks since I saw her last. And I've been at a conference in the meantime. In fact, I just returned this afternoon."

"Well, I'm glad you were home and able to get this."

"Thanks a lot, Lola, I will look at it when I have time," he said as he shut the door behind her.

What could this be, he thought as he walked back into the living room. I'll get to it later, after I get unpacked tomorrow and settled back into my routines. He then forgot about it completely, being a busy man, and a well-known physician to boot. The next time he ran across Miss Martin in his office records, he discovered again that she had died, and was reminded of Lola's visit a month or two earlier. Where was the document she had given him? He had no idea.

* * *

"What is this?" Vicki asked when she got to the bottom of the stairs. "I was collecting the trash and found it in the wastebasket of your study mixed in with old bills and advertisements." She sounded angry.

He looked at the opened envelope marked "Strictly Confidential." "So you found it! I got this a while back and forgot about it entirely until recently! I wondered what had happened to it," he answered.

"It looks like you had an affair recently if I get the drift of the text in this memoir. I'm not in a forgiving mood, so can you explain this to me?"

"I haven't read the thing yet! Let me see it so I can read it for the first time."

Vicki thrust the so-called memoir at him angrily, and stomped off. Arthur was chagrined even before he read it, knowing Vicki's moods could be stern, almost violent. It was not the first time she had opened his personal mail.

He read the memoir in its entirety. It was brief, written on 3 x 5 cards, all undated, which made it difficult to keep track. It began and ran on in the following way:

I loved him from the first time I saw him. I first met him as an intern named Dr. Helmsford while still in training. I knew that he would develop into a good doctor, and that he had a good future in front of him. He was so kind on my first visit, when he found the lump in my right breast. It was nothing to worry about, he told me, and he later excised it under the supervision of a senior doctor. He was careful that way, and I loved him all the more because of that. At another physical exam ten years later, the physician in charge of me discovered that another lump in my breast had metastasized to my brain, all unseen and unfelt by me. I was very ignorant at the time and didn't know what to think of this problem, except to see Dr. Helmsford again. I looked him up on the Internet, and found that he was working then at MGH nearby. This was fortunate, because at the age of 40, I still loved him, and looked forward to seeing him again, serious as my condition was. I was right in my instincts. He looked older and wearier. But when I saw the letters stenciled on his pocket tag identifying him as Dr. Helmsford, I was overjoyed to see him again, and said so immediately. I felt I was in good hands again. During the initial paperwork, I had to tell him about the discovery of the metastasis, and he looked stricken to hear it. He moved quickly to confirm the diagnosis with the help of CT and MRI scans that had become available in the meantime. He had me admitted to the hospital and came by to see me every day. I hoped to marry Dr. Helmsford someday, but my

*days were getting short, owing to my cancerous condition.
Knowing that I had but a short time to live I realized this
was unlikely. But I could at least hope for an engagement
before the end. To my infinite pleasure and gratitude this
took place in my hospital room, sitting side by side on the
edge of the bed. It was Dr. Helmsford and myself together,
with two witnesses to make it semi-legal. The witnesses
turned a private moment into a rite of solemnity. This was a
moment of triumph for me; I had accomplished all I could
have wished for.*

The memoir was illegible from here on, and try as he
might, Arthur could make nothing of it. He could see why
Vicki was upset at reading this document, but was perplexed
at her anger. Surely she could see that it was pure fantasy. He
realized he would need to confront her and discuss this with
her—the sooner the better.

He went to the family room and sat down across from her.

"I've read the document you assaulted me with, and I can
see why you were so disturbed by it. But it's a pure work
of imagination—a fantasy. She had brain cancer, for heaven's
sake. It's the equivalent of transference, as psychologists think
of it, where the doctor takes on a holy character in the patient's
eyes. When a patient is as ill as this one, is it surprising that
the doctor would take on an almost biblical character to her?"

"I'm not convinced," Vicki said, more calmly now. "Do you
remember the time when we were about to be engaged when
you slept with your old girlfriend 'one last time'? It offended

me terribly, as you may remember, and I almost called off the engagement."

"Don't bring *that* up now. It has nothing to do with this memoir." It was hard to remember this incident, since it happened many years ago, and Arthur preferred to forget it for obvious reasons.

"It's true, you confessed immediately," Vicki conceded, "but that hasn't allowed me to forget, much less forgive you."

Arthur sighed. "Let's drop the whole subject. I am sick of being reminded of it." Vicki pretended not to hear this and got up and walked off without displaying her previous anger. But Arthur could tell it was still alive.

* * *

The next time Arthur saw Lola—she still worked on the same floor—he was tempted to tell her of the divorce proceedings going on with Vicki. They were in the cafeteria, carrying trays, and he asked if he could join her. He had few friends with whom he could speak about intimate matters.

"Lola, I think I'm headed for divorce from Vicki. I'm sorry to tell you this, but the trigger has to do with something you know about. Remember the document you gave me after Miss Martin died? I'm embarrassed to say I lost it for a while before I had even read it because I was so busy after coming back from my conference. I frankly forgot about it until Vicki found it in my wastebasket. I must accidentally have tossed it out with old bills and other stuff from my desk. Vicki read it before I had a chance to do so, and it revealed Miss Martin's deep affection for me, which I still can't understand."

"Dr. Helmsford, everybody knew Miss Martin was in love with you."

He looked at her in total disbelief. "That's ridiculous. I hardly noticed her as a person, except for her condition. If she did have feelings about me they must have been brought on by her brain cancer."

Lola interrupted him and said, "Don't you remember: I was one of the witnesses at your so-called engagement ceremony! I know you did it only out of the goodness of your heart." She smiled at him. "It was so sweet of you, it almost made *me* fall in love with you."

SAY ANYTHING

"Honey, do my straps show in back?"

"Not a bit, but the cleavage in front is stunning."

"I don't have to believe you, but thanks."

"Do believe me, it's the fi rst thing I noticed about you a year ago."

"OK I believe you Do you think Mona is pretty?"

"Well, yes. Though she's a little strong for my taste. But very nice, very handsome. Dave is a lucky man."

"Do you feel lucky, honey?"

"Of course I do, dear. Don't you?"

"Yes. Your tie needs straightening."

"Thanks. Move from the mirror for a sec."

"And your shoe could use a wipe."

"Thanks. You've been seeing a lot of the Lamberts, Lindy. You must enjoy them."

"Not really, just Mona. She's interesting and right next door. I don't think they're getting on very well."

"What makes you think so?"

"The way she doesn't talk about him."

"Why should she? Do you talk about me when you see her during the day?"

"Well, not much. We have our woman thing when we're alone."

"So what do women talk about? I've always wondered. When I listen, they never seem to take turns."

"Just life, parents, things like that. Whether to have kids. She said you were really an attractive, nice guy."

"That's because of my extreme modesty and good looks. But it's mainly 'hello, nice day' with her. I see Dave more often, but he's sort of closed. He doesn't pick up on my chattiness and wit. But I can't help being a friendly fellow."

"I know that from experience. It's why I'm living with you now."

"I'm the lucky one, dear. I hope you feel as lucky."

"Well, yes. We've been over that before."

"What do you mean? Is my tie OK now?"

"I mean like I said you're the only guy I was really attracted to. The few others, you know, left me kind of bored."

"Sex is complicated. You're the best, a sailor's dream."

"Come on, Colin, you've said that a hundred times, three of them to me."

"What can I say?"

"Do you think I'm passionate enough?"

"In my book, Venus is a frump. You're it. I love the way you let me take the lead. Do you really enjoy it?"

"Of course. I want you to have the best."

"I have the best. You're a sexy angel."

"What do you see in Mona? She's a sexier angel than I am."

"Get off it, Lindy. I don't see anything in Mona. She may look sexy, and maybe she is, but how would I know? In fact, how would you know?"

"Honey, we've got to get moving. Even though they're just next door. I don't think they're expecting anyone else."

"Your whim is my command. Give me a toilet paper for my shoe. You look nervous."

"I'm not nervous, Colin, just wondering if this is going to work."

"I don't follow. What work?"

"You and me. Do you see Mona when I'm away?"

"Not unless she comes outdoors. What are you after?"

"Colin. There's never a right time. I want to know if she was ever, you know, friendly with you."

"Lindy, no. She's attractive and I'm a man and what can I say? But she seems totally uninterested in me. As her best friend, you should know that from all the woman talk you two do."

"So you've tested the waters, right?"

"I didn't say that. She comes across as a friendly neighbor, that's all. What's going on? Why are you taking off your necklace? We've got to go."

"We're not going. Colin, I don't know how to say it except to say it. Mona and I are in love. It just came out on Monday, and...and...Neither of us felt this way before."

"Holy shit. Why now?"

"Call them, Colin. Say anything."

WHERE'S JULIA?

"Ooh, Honey, something's in there!"

It was hard to know whether it was the end of a dream or Julia calling from the bathroom. I didn't hear anything else. That meant it was a dream. Keep it simple. I went back to sleep.

Julia is not in bed beside me when I wake up. Or in the bathroom. The morning silence is familiar after all. The sun is up over the neighbor's roof, and for a while I get the dewy smell of grass in the room. The sunlight lies in bands along the floor between the shadows of the miniblind slats. The sun highlights the dust on the slats, giving them a fuzzy look. Soon I would get up and get the day going, as my mother used to say. The folds in Julia's blue pillowcase are the only other thing I can see as I lie on my side. Morning is almost the only time I can lie still and do nothing. He says relax, just think. I do that in the morning, looking at things that are right before my eyes, like the pillowcase and its hem and the threads that I can almost count, crossing each other. I always wonder how cotton pillowcases, or linens, for that matter, are made. They are so dense with tiny, crossing threads you would think the machines would have very tiny whatevers that pack them so closely. They should be more expensive, the sheets. I'll look that up. Maybe today. I'll get that on the tentative list. That comes later, though. Now it is time to get up, close the window behind the fuzzy blinds, pee, brush the old teeth, which are yellowing even though I use whitening toothpaste. *Consumers* says it's the best, even though it's the cheapest. It's not doing the job, but it doesn't matter. I go in and brush my hair, put on my robe. The robe is red. Dr. McTeague joked that I will be easier to find that way. He's like that, he's a nice person.

Then I go into the kitchen. Before breakfast I start a list of things to do, like I do every day. On my yellow legal pad. It's still hard to get it right the first time. Shop for food with Dinah. Get the wire wheeled cart. No, get the cart, then go with her to shop for food. I rearrange the list to get it right. All of this after waiting for Dinah, my case worker. And while waiting, answer e-mail, starting with complaints from clients, clients unhappy with my advice about investments. Investments that we even hold in our own portfolio. I would get information. Internet and some phone calls.

I'm getting way ahead of myself. I tear off the sheet and start a new list, keeping the old one for reference. First, start breakfast, which I am already doing. Then get dressed. Actually, I should have done that before breakfast, or I would be in my robe and slippers all day. There is room at the head of the paper on my legal pad to put that in, dressing. Just under the place where it is bound and perforated. But I am already making breakfast, if you can call it that. An English muffin and orange juice. I pull the halves of the muffin apart. I enjoy them more when they come apart easily, releasing a fresh bread smell. I put them in the toaster. Even so, I could still dress before breakfast, so while the muffin is toasting I go back to the bedroom and put on my old clothes. I don't have to shave, so that won't be on the list. I go back to the kitchen.

The muffin is done. Perfectly. Butter is all I use. The cat eats in the evening, and that goes way at the bottom of the page. Julia will do that. Feed the cat in the evening. Whiskas.

If Julia doesn't come back, and I guess she won't, it's all up to me. I can just make dinner for myself, which I write down on the list after the cat. Luckily I'd left space for that. I reflect that with Julia gone, life is not much more trouble because I did most of these things before anyway. She is a very busy woman. It is just a matter of keeping lists now, very satisfying to check off. I just have to remember to have the cat near the end of the list. And I've already written that down. And speaking of the cat, a nondescript tabby that adopted us in the summer, she hasn't shown up in the morning like she usually does. Her name was Tiger. Is Tiger. Tiger is probably with Julia, so I don't worry. Tiger is really Julia's cat. But it is too early to take feeding Tiger off the list. I can wait. It's better to wait and see whether plans really have to change or not. You can never be sure.

Dr. McTeague gives me contradictory directions. He wants me to keep thinking, maybe go for a walk or listen to music. Just relax and see what you can remember, whether you can remember. He says I've been coming around, getting much better oriented. He said that when I told him about how finding my way around the kitchen, getting breakfast, was so much easier. In fact, that's what this experiment of coming home is all about. It's been two weeks now. I know because I keep my lists and date them. When I leave, he says next time tell me what you did. Tell me about your days. Naturally, I don't want to leave things out when I see him. My lists are very helpful for that very reason. So I save them. No, he says, make notes at the end of the day on what you've already done. Not on what you'll do later. You don't even have to remember most of the things on these lists, he says. Very contradictory. Anyway, days are very rewarding with a good plan.

So back to the list. I finish my muffin and the sun is really up now, introducing a warm day, but I don't go out. Even though I'm dressed. I remember to put looking up linen on the right hand side. That's where tentative plans go, but they have to be down on the page about the place they will belong if I get around to them. Then all I need is an arrow to show where they go. Any free time is useful for things like that. Next thing is to boot up. No, it's getting a cup of coffee, which means getting my favorite cup from the study first. I remember it is there from yesterday. That didn't need to be on the list, because it's part of getting coffee itself. Some things we don't have to break down into separate tasks. Dr. McTeague says that's progress. But earlier, I found that problem solving, especially the most difficult problems, can be done much more easily that way. When Jackson & Duffy were in real trouble, they came to me to see how their mortgage portfolio could make a profit. Instead of incurring losses. You would think someone would be monitoring the business better, but I said to Sidney, who had just taken over real estate, "Sid, increase the variable rate as soon as the index goes up. Make sure you enforce the prepayment penalty. Foreclose the duds after two months, not six. And don't believe everything you hear. Research clients better from now on." Just like that. Sidney did all those things and now—or then, whatever—that side of the business is in the black. It's one of those things I remember with pride. I recommended Sid for my position when I moved up. He took over Trusts when I became a vice president. It was a long time ago, though. So I guess it's coffee and then boot up. They call it booting up from the expression raising yourself by your bootstraps. Think of it. A computer, all cold, knows what to do when you turn it on. It's ready for you in a minute or two, maybe less.

I have just enough room on my legal pad to put coffee and booting between breakfast and e-mail. Stupid of me not to see you have to boot up before e-mail. Whatever Dr. McTeague says, you can see it's good to have a list. I went over to legal pads because my lists get longer every day. He says not to give in or ignore it, try to remember. Make a list of what you remember. I put on the list to make time to remember. It would have to come after the clients. Actually, I don't have clients any more. I wonder how that got on the list. Actually, now that I'm at it, Dr. McTeague might have a point. Let's see if I can remember some of them, clients. I should get on the computer, after it boots up, of course, and see if I can go back to the records. They're in the Jackson & Duffy site, very secure. Password, passcode. No. I will be denied access, I remember now. So that won't work. Stupid of me to forget to remember I was retired. Medically.

I brew the coffee, a habit I enjoy. Put the coffee grounds, three cups worth, into the paper cone. After the cone goes into the Mr. Coffee, of course, then the water, which comes from the decanter, which is filled at the sink. The paper cones are hard to separate with one hand, but I've gotten very good at that. Then the smell of the coffee as it drains into the decanter makes me feel more alert. Before I've drunk a drop. I do all that. And then, to cut a long story short, I go with a cup of coffee, sugar, no cream, to the study and turn on the computer.

I should have done that while the coffee was brewing, but no matter, they are done in the right order. One thing at a time. And once the various boots come and go on the screen, my e-mail automatically comes on. It's AOL.com and like always it says 'You've got mail!' The exclamation point makes me feel like a real person. I get a kick out of it even though it's all, the e-mail, what they call spam. When I came home I had what must have been a thousand e-mails, and I couldn't read them all. I don't know how they came to call unwanted e-mail spam. Viagra, investments (my old business), interesting propositions from Africa, which I actually had to tell my clients to ignore, Macy's, tours, many charities. And discounted books. And today, what do I see but a message from Dr. McTeague! There it is, a rare message from mct@psclin.umn.edu. My word, as my mother used to say, this is a privilege.

McTeague. Now I look at my weekly calendar on another pad. It's blue, not yellow, so they won't get mixed up. I now see and remember that I will meet with him this afternoon. 2:30 p.m. Dinah will take me there and we'll shop on the way back. My list is getting messy, but by writing small, I get it all in there. I should have put looking at my calendar first on my yellow list, even before getting dressed, which I had to do, it turns out, even before breakfast. The one thing about having a case worker is that she brings the pills, and I don't have to remember them or put them on the list. When she comes, it's the first thing. I tell Dr. McTeague that even Dinah keeps a list. It's on a clipboard, and she writes a lot down. She never lets me see what she writes, but I'm sure it's about my progress. I won't forget whether I have taken them, the pills, or not. Actually, I probably will, but it won't matter because I will have. Taken them. Dinah will see to that. I should not have waited to start my list until breakfast. Or before breakfast. Or getting dressed, whatever.

Dr. McTeague says in his email message, "I thought I might reach you this way, and that's one thing I'll know when we meet today. But before you begin other things, turn your computer off, get comfortable with a pencil and paper and see what you can remember about Julia. It would be very helpful to us if you could remember. Go into the bathroom and just see what you can remember." I started two weeks ago by using a pen for my lists, but I needed something with an eraser.

Julia. One thing is sure, she isn't here, even in the bathroom. But is someone else? She took Tiger to wherever she went. But first, I have to erase all the spam, being careful not to erase important messages like Dr. McTeague's and some that require more reading than I'm ready to do now. I find reading on a computer screen difficult, probably because of the way I sit forward in my desk chair. But a few of these are interesting, and I don't want to waste paper printing them out, so I save them till later. If I erase all the unimportant things, the ones that are left will actually be a list right there on the computer so I don't have to write them down on the legal pad, the yellow one. Saves work, saves paper. But I do put on my list to go back to e-mail later. After the appointment with Dr. McTeague. And shopping with Dinah.

About Julia. I went through all that before with Dr. McTeague, about how I met her in business school. And marrying her after I got my first position. With a bank, no less. She became a teller. It was a small bank, much smaller than Jackson & Duffy. I think we had fun. I'm sure of it, we didn't have any children. But Tiger came to us in the summer. Years later. That—I mean Tiger—was all I could really handle, with all my work. I was very good at work, as Sid would tell you if you met him and asked him. He's gone now, no one really knows where. Dr. McTeague reminded me. Just last week. A Mr. Langston takes care of things now. I was in the Trust department, managing dead peoples' savings for the benefit of widows and children. Not for many widowers, though, since they die early. I mean, before their wives. In fact, they don't know they won't be widowers till they're dead, if then.

I write some of this down for Dr. McTeague, but I'd told him about all these things before and he didn't need to hear them again. Or see them again, on my notes of what I remember. I tried to think about Julia. Julia. Where was she, after all? Last night she was somewhere, out of bed when I had that dream. I thought it was a dream, but Julia would know, she was there. She said something was there. Where? In the bathroom? I should have written that down right then, but it's hard in the dark. Impossible, really. I make a note about that now to show Dr. McTeague. He often asks about the bathroom, but I don't really remember, it seems to have happened so fast. He asks did I see anything in the shower? I know now that I just went back to sleep, so of course I couldn't tell him anything about that. Or the police, who keep asking who was there. Julia was always saying she wanted children and couldn't wait much longer. And I was injured so badly, but not much blood, in a coma for a week or two. Or three, maybe longer. They say Dinah found me, when she came to clean. It would seem Julia just plain disappeared if she and Tiger don't come back tonight. Even her clothes are gone. At the dry cleaners? They haven't told me everything. I mean Dr.

McTeague and the police. What I do is run a trust department caring for widows and children. Actually, I don't any more since I retired and Sid took over. Actually, Sid took over, then I retired. No, Sid took over, then he left and I became vice president even before I retired. Anyway, when he left, Mr. Langston took over our family trust, mine and Julia's. I'm sorry Sid left the firm, because he and Julia worked so well together, and I didn't have to worry about it at all. The trust, I mean. Mr. Langston arranged for Dinah to come every day, and he will act for a while as a conservator. Depending on how my recovery goes. And depending on whether they can contact Sid, who left months ago. He's the only one who would be able to iron out the transfers Julia made somewhere foreign out of our portfolio. Julia would know, since everything in the trust was in her hands when I became vice president. And as I said, it's not so odd that there are relatively few widowers. There's a few, and who knows, I may be one of the lucky ones. Someday, you never know. Whatever, Sid said that Julia will be well taken care of. I'll have to put on the list to ask Dr. McTeague where he thinks Julia went. He's always asking me about Julia, so we'll just have to put our heads together. I'm sure Sid knows, if they can locate him. Even if they can't.

LYDIA

I won't go into it now, but I always thought Jay was a fraud. He would say something like "I'm going to New York for the weekend," and then not go. He would remain at home, contented to be there, oblivious to the fact that he had said he would be away.

As a discontented housewife, I could no longer stand it, so I decided to take matters into my own hands. I thought that it might be good to apply reverse pressure on him by lying to him. I decided to say, on short notice, "C'mon honey, would you like to join me in San Francisco?" I had absolutely no intention of going to San Francisco. I planned to just stay in our house in Boston until he asked about the trip, which he never did.

This was the way I discovered he had Alzheimer's. This discovery shocked me. We were in our late sixties (to tell the truth, he was in his early seventies), and moderately well-off, and it was now up to me to take care of financial affairs and keep up with the bills. I had a lot of practice at this, because I had been keeping the books for a long time, and so this was not new to me.

I now had a husband with Alzheimer's, but I was still a housewife after all, and idle—and bored. I will not go into the whole story, but the fact is, I decided to go shopping in hopes that this would distract me. I was sure that Jay was in good hands, owing to the people that provided 24/7 care for him. I then went shopping for goods that I didn't need—cheap, but serviceable—and that amused me. They included a spatula, a 3D Motorola television set, and four hamsters from the pet store. Oh yes, and on another outing, I bought a Porsche Carrera Cabriolet, which depleted our savings of $85,000, as I later discovered. I was happy as a clam, to which I bore no small resemblance. In the years that followed, I was aging, and followed the routine to which I had become accustomed. I'm not sure what happened to Jay or to his care-takers, but they casually dropped out of my life. On occasional shopping trips I would become lost, but thought nothing of it.

The next thing I knew, I was really lost and didn't know where I was. I ultimately found my way home, though home looked different than I remembered it. I finally forgave Jay for his many indiscretions.

FRIENDS AND FAMILY

CRAFTSMAN

For as long as I can remember, my father was a very gifted craftsman. At the age of seven years, he would make a nicely beveled cardboard box in minutes. He went on to make crafted tables out of nothing special when he was just in his teens. When he was grown, he became a superb fashioner of furniture with all the tools of the trade: planes, lathes, drills, saws (both rotary and Skill Saws), routers and all. He married and had a child (me) and went into business for himself.

I missed my mother greatly after she died of lung cancer when I was sixteen years of age. As a result I continued to live with my father. I was going to a nearby university so I could commute easily. This not only saved money but helped my father greatly in dealing with his loneliness. Later, I was employed at a local newspaper of which I became editor, and began to build a life of my own. But I remained close to my father and continued to follow his work as a craftsman.

Although I enjoyed a partnership for many years, I never married, and so stayed close to my father and visited him often. I watched as he worked on his projects and was amazed at his progress, particularly in view of his age. He worked on one particular coffee table in ways that intrigued me. He first hollowed out a space for the legs, which he then carved with a complex design. Once the basic structure was completed, he sanded the top, making sure there was room for an upturned barrier, so things would not slide off the table edge when it was finished. This was a nice touch, but difficult for him. He worked on this table off and on, between other projects. As it neared completion, I was living with him again, and still enjoyed watching his carpentry. He was getting increasingly infirm and the work got slower and slower. Nevertheless, he continued to work on the table until it was done, and by this time, he was eighty.

He had carved from this hard wood a beautiful table, with lion's feet holding balls for support, curved legs, a well-molded apron. The top, bordered with a subtle raised lip, curved gracefully from corner to corner. He oiled the wood, polished it carefully and with my help brought it in and placed it before his divan with pride. "Now it's yours," he said.

As he said this he placed a beer bottle on the table, where it left a ring. "Now we can say it's been used." He lifted his rheumy eyes to me, clouded with years of close work on his table. "Be sure you use coasters now."

Soon he was unable to rise from the divan without my help. The divan sagged as he sat behind the table for a few more years, sinking further into contented forgetfulness and finally death itself. I always use a coaster, but I never cover the beer bottle ring he left as a signature.

SWAN

Since I was four, I considered myself an ugly duckling. My hair grew in straight, and my lips were too thick for anyone to call me beautiful. Moreover, I was too thin—excessively so—for people to call me cute.

Besides this, I was naturally shy and didn't make friends easily owing to a series of tragedies in my family. First, my brother died of diphtheria when he was seven. Because I was the younger sister by one year, I was forgotten in the process of my parents' grieving for him. I could not fault my parents for this, but I did. I adored my brother excessively—first, because he was a year older, and next, because he was much smarter. I felt abandoned at that age, and I both hated him for dying, and missed him very much. It didn't help that my parents doted on him excessively for a long time after he died.

Second, as I grew up, I became aware of how heartbroken my mother still was over the death of Julian (that was my brother's name). I caught her once when I was twelve tippling whiskey in secret in the pantry, and it was the first inkling that she had become an alcoholic. I said nothing to my father about this, because I was still innocent about such things. When my mother's drinking became intolerable, my father became more and more withdrawn. He was not a good father to me in the interim.

As I learned later, he was aware from the beginning of her drinking on the sly, but he couldn't do anything about it. After a spat over my mother's drinking and driving, which I overheard and which upset me, he simply gave up. In spite of this, my mother continued driving for a while to go shopping for groceries and apparel when she felt sober enough to do so. But it got so bad that my father finally put his foot down and no longer permitted her to drive. Not only did he expressly forbid my mother to drive, he tried to prevent it by keeping the keys to the car in his pocket. She found them when he mistakenly mislaid them on the piano. He always regretted this mistake, because she was drunk at the time. Unhappily, she died in an accident that day while she was still intoxicated.

.

My father remarried a coworker from the office where he worked when I was fifteen. My stepmother turned out to be kind and raised, me, her new stepdaughter, as her own. She would groom my hair for a half hour after I took a shower. She would do my make-up for me, careful to make my lips look thinner. She also took care for me to gain weight until I was quite beautiful. She noted my breasts when they emerged, and told me how to handle my periods when they finally came. I reveled in the attention, because I was the object of so much care, which she considered her own creation. I shared her pride in this transformation too. After having learned to make myself up, I took special care to make myself look as stunning as my stepmother did, studying beauty magazines and ads for the products that would help. In the end, I was a thing of beauty, and felt I should hide my satisfaction from my friends, of whom I had few. I took on a new nickname for myself: 'Swan', which I used only with my closest friends.

"She's nothing but a spoiled brat," I overheard one of my closest friends say, when she thought I was out of earshot.

UNCLE VANYA

My uncle 'Vanya,' as I called him, lost his wife of many years quite suddenly to a heart attack. (I called him this based on his surname, Vanderven.) Because we had room for him we decided to take him in. He started living with my parents and me in a three-bedroom house in a tony part of town. At first, he was welcomed to our family with open arms, despite the small inconveniences it entailed. Like having me move into another room, or adjust my breakfast schedule to accommodate Uncle Vanya and still get to school on time. I was six at the time of Vanya's moving in with us.

As I grew up, we (my parents and I) had no trouble to have Vanya as part of our lives because he remained silent much of the time. We noticed an occasional whimper once in a while, but we tended to ignore this except to comfort him when he was clearly in psychological pain. We didn't know the reason for the whimper; but it seemed to hide a mystery deep in his soul.

Before I went to college, I was determined to find out what it was that was bothering him. He would talk occasionally, but not often, mainly at social gatherings. People who had known Vanya for some time were used to his behavior and thought nothing further of it. But I was curious about what was bothering him in his long silences. I was nervous about asking openly about this unusual trait and worried for some weeks how to broach this. One day I got up the nerve to ask him about it and to my complete surprise, he answered at length.

"You must know," he began, "that I was completely in love with a girl, Odette, in my youth, and it got me into a lot of trouble. I got her pregnant without benefit of marriage, and after nine months a child was born. I was not present at or after the birth, since she was suffering from various complications, including postpartum depression."

Vanya looked at me and took a deep breath. "The child was *you*," he said. "I suspect you don't realize that I am your father. Your mother left the hospital without telling me because she was still very depressed. Your parents kindly took you in as a newborn. They felt they had no choice, being the only other living relatives you had. They formally adopted you as their own, and the rest is history. They took me in years later, as you know, and I can't tell you how happy I have been to be here. Thank your parents, and God, for that."

He paused for a moment. "I am no longer looking for Odette, despite being in love with her still. That's why I cry occasionally when I'm alone." Vanya began crying again, and could not stop until I comforted him with sympathetic pats on the shoulder.

"I had no idea of my true origin," I told him, when he had calmed down. "What you told me is a revelation. I've got to think about this before I tell my 'parents' what you have told me." I was stunned at this news.

"So your parents did not tell you? I thought they might have, but asked you not to let me know so as not to burden me."

"I was obviously too young at the time my parents adopted me," I said. "And they may have wanted to spare me any anxiety about my past."

"I hope I did not do wrong by telling you," Vanya said.

I shook my head. "It's no matter now that we know. I hope that you feel better now that the story is out. And I feel no different after all these years. I'm just glad that your burden is hopefully lifted. And, as I say, it's insignificant now, at least to me."

Alone, I thought about this for some time, and felt again that the revelation was not significant anymore. It was good to have it resolved, and so it bothered me less and less. Until recently.

I was thirty-one and getting curious about my birth mother's existence. It was a long time since I had thought about her. I suppose it is natural for a person of my age to become curious at last. How does one find someone who has been lost for so many years? I decided to become a detective, searching for Odette's whereabouts. First I looked for any correspondence about my adoption and found documents relating to the event in an old file cabinet, forgotten by my parents. In the bottom drawer of the same cabinet, I found a small packet of letters of correspondence relating to the event. To my surprise, some were from Odette. She was evidently good at covering her tracks, and in the last letter to my parents assured them she was fine, about to be married, and implored them not to contact her again. That was the last letter in the file. I therefore gave up my search, thinking that it was best to let sleeping dogs lie. If Uncle Vanya had tried to find her, surely he could have talked to my parents about this. This would have allowed him to look for her at her last address or trace her from there if he still loved her so much.

But in the end I was still troubled about the matter, and decided to confront Vanya—no longer *Uncle* Vanya—about it again.

"I have to ask you something," I told him. "You told me that you stopped looking for Odette. But it sounds as though you did look for her for a time?"

"No," he said. "I stopped looking for her after I married my wife. I knew by then that Odette too had married, and it was unfair to both spouses to keep looking for her"

"So we'll never know what happened to Odette?"

"No," he said. "But I have an old picture of her if you would like to see it." He rummaged through his few belongings and came up with an old photograph of Odette as a teenager. She was lovely and I could see why Vanya had fallen in love with her. I wondered if I looked like her.

And that was the last discussion I had with Uncle Vanya or anyone else on the subject. However, I have no regrets. The conversations I had with him taught me a great deal about marriage. I only hope that I can find similar happiness in mine, whenever that happens.

ON STAGE

Benjamin was the son of an actor who grew up in thrall to his father's profession. When his father was on tour, he would turn himself to reading. His mother filled in when the father was on tour and encouraged him. He was in love with words from the time he could read. He read the youthful works of Dr. Seuss when he was a child, and *Moby Dick* when he was a teenager. Later, he read Shakespeare, and all of the classics he could lay his hands on. When his voice changed, he discovered that he had become a rich bass. His father, being an actor, took great pride in his son's developing interests.

Benjamin had a sister eight years older than he was. Her name was Kate. He did not get along with her from an early age. He was in the habit, when he got older, of calling her 'hateful Kate' or better yet, 'hateful Kateful'. She was always telling him what to do and telling him to stop talking so much. It was a great relief when she went to college. He could then read without interruption. Benjamin's parents felt his dislike of his sister was a simple case of sibling rivalry, and forgot about it once Kate left for college.

When Benjamin reached the age of twenty-two, he discovered that his mother was dying of cancer. This was a surprise to him because he had no forewarning of her condition. His mother had kept it a secret for some years, but the truth finally came out. She died soon afterwards, and Benjamin was heartbroken. He really didn't know what to do with himself. Kate was finished with college and had subsequently gotten married, leaving Benjamin free to do anything befitting his talents. In talking to his father one day, his father suggested he come with him to the theater. He was encouraged to do prop work and shortly thereafter became a bit part player in productions starring his father. His father recognized the potential of his voice, which could vary from bass to alto and suggested that he go to drama school. There was no one at home to care for, and the success of the father's career provided sufficient funds to pay for acting lessons.

Benjamin's talents were recognized immediately by some famous theaters, including one on Broadway. He was given the role of the son Biff in *Death of a Salesman*, for which he was well suited. This led to a role of the gentleman caller in *The Glass Menagerie* by Tennessee Williams and he improved from that point on. It was a fast process, and it seemed overnight that he became famous, owing chiefly to his voice, which became downright musical with time. Soon he was offered the role of Hamlet, which he played for several years on tour. He became an international success. He enjoyed the fame this brought him despite the death of his father at the age of eighty.

Benjamin drew from his heart shades of humanity more varied than all tragedians before him. He learned languages and accents, poses and telling gestures that invested Lear and Loman, Oedipus, Cyrano, and Don Juan with unprecedented authenticity. He lived clothed in his creations, spoke with their voices, entered their exalted lives.

A stroke deprived Benjamin of speech. His sister, Kate, looked in on him occasionally, because her husband had died, and her children were grown. He was fonder of Kate than he had been before but he had no way of telling her. His characters lived on in pantomime in his mind. He longed to present them, present himself again to the world, but he had no words even to understand his loss. Even as he failed his models, he shared their tragedies.

A WORD TO THE WISE

I'll never forget my father saying to me, 'a word to the wise, son'. He would repeat this every time I got into trouble as a child through some daring exploit or other. I could hear him say this before he even uttered a word. He'd go on to say, "You've been a naughty boy, and you should listen to your father." I would listen, but he would never say anything more or ever punish me. I took satisfaction in that. As a result, I became more daring than ever.

I was indeed a daring child, climbing trees beyond my abilities, going into other people's garages to investigate what was in there, and hanging out in other places where I didn't belong.

My father was a skilled doctor, specializing in infant heart difficulties. He was thanked by many mothers who sent him gifts for years after their child's birth. His name was George Mason, and he was best known for delicate operations shortly after a child's birth. He took great pride in his achievements, and became famous as a result. He was known especially for his development of techniques to close holes in imperfect hearts that led to poor circulation of the blood.

I, on the other hand, remained a daring child and kept this reputation for a good part of my life. I acquired the nickname 'Reckless Richard,' which suited me to a T. As I grew up, I took all kinds of chances with odd-tasting food, trees (I learned how to scale some of the highest in the neighborhood), and lumber, believe it or not. One of my projects in my teens was to build a tree-house from leftover lumber that was lying around unfinished houses. I would take it at night when no one was looking. I never got caught doing this, and showing the finished result to close friends was a source of great pride to me. In fact, I took as much pleasure in this as my father did in his heart work.

I then considered what I would do as an adult. Something risky, perhaps. Something dangerous, like robbing banks? Or becoming a stuntman? I decided on the latter, because it wouldn't run me afoul of the law. After that it was "Hollywood here I come!" I set out for Hollywood with high hopes, and landed a good job almost immediately—after demonstrating that I could fall off horses with acrobatic ease, and suffer explosions without serious damage to my person. I made a substantial salary, because I was so able in the profession. I worked with John Wayne, Tom Mix, and others of note, including some women I very much admired. I became the lover of one who praised my ability as a stuntman, always walking away with no injuries to speak of. Actually, I did sustain one major injury that sent me to the hospital, but it did not impair my lovemaking as I discovered when my love visited me.

Years later, when my father was in his dotage, he suffered a stroke. He was inarticulate, but I visited him often. It was then that I remembered his saying, 'A word to the wise, son.' So I said, "A word to the wise, Dad." I really had no wisdom to impart, just as he had never really imparted any to me. I was glad that neither of us ever produced a "sufficient" word. It left us both free to be ourselves.

SMALL TALK

"Hello, Marcia. It's good to see you again. How've you been?"

"Oh! Not so good, considering everything that's happened."

"Tell me about it, Marcia. It sounds like you've had a lot of trouble."

"Would you like to have some coffee, Celeste? I would have the liberty to tell you my sad story at length. I'm free now, because I've finished my shopping."

"So have I, Marcia. Let's do it."

* * *

"I haven't seen you since your babies were born," said Celeste, after they had settled into a booth at the coffee shop. "I don't know where the time goes, or where the friends go, for all I know."

"Neither do I," said Marcia. "It seems to be a condition of motherhood. You lose touch with friends, especially if you move out of the neighborhood." Marcia took a sip of her coffee before she got down to business. "You wanted to hear my sad story, since I got married. Do you want the long or the short version?"

"I'll have the long version. This is a good opportunity to catch up with you," answered Celeste. "I'm as free as a bird and have nothing more to do all day."

"I'm relieved. I have so much to tell you. First of all, I was married as you know, and shortly before that, my husband had an affair with an ex-girlfriend. We worked it out, I thought successfully, but doubts then continued to increase in my mind. Shortly after the birth of the twins, it happened again with the same girlfriend. I knew because he told me, and things were not the same after that. I was thinking about divorce but I had the twins to take care of, and it seemed difficult for all of us. Also, I had a good house to live in, and that too made it impractical from my standpoint. So we live together—and still do—but not intimately if you know what I mean. I'm frustrated, of course, and I have no idea what he does on the weekends when he is away 'on business'. But of course I can image what kind of business keeps him busy."

"I can understand how this must disturb you," Celeste put in. "I couldn't do that myself. If it were me, I would get out of the marriage entirely. Of course, it's easy for me to say that since I'm pretty well off on account of my job and my husband."

"Sometimes I feel like murdering him. But at others, I know he takes good care of the children, and I'm grateful for that, especially when I'm busy with my own job, which I do at home. I know he feels guilty as hell, but what can I do?"

"I would opt for the former," Celeste said, "if I were not charged for it. I'm sure you can find an understanding lawyer." She smiled as she said this.

Marcia and Celeste finished their coffee and parted on good terms. They said goodbye to one another, promising to keep in touch.

* * *

Celeste's telephone rang and it was Marcia. It had been over a year since they had met at the coffee shop. "I've got big news for you. You have time now? Can we get together?"

"Yes, of course, for you, any time," Celeste answered. "I would love to hear your news, especially if it's of major interest. Come on over, and I'll put on some coffee."

An hour later they were settled in Celeste's living room before the fireplace, sipping espresso out of tiny cups.

"Let me start at the beginning. First of all, I've gotten a divorce, and the good news is that I can keep the house. The semi-bad news is that I've lost custody of the children. It was only semi-bad, because my husband was fonder of them than I was, I think. I have my regrets, but not many. We got married too early, and that's what I regret most. We worked this out by mutual agreement, few lawyers—nothing complicated."

"This must have happened fast," Celeste said after a deep breath. "I can't believe what I just heard."

"We decided this soon after you and I had our coffee-shop talk at the mall last year. It was simple because I didn't want to murder him and divorce was the better more legal option. He enjoys the kids and I love the freedom of my life now. Also, I've met his former ex-girlfriend, who turned out to be very nice, and likes the girls very much. Her name is Jennifer and I have to confess that she is more appropriate for him than I ever was. On my regular bimonthly visits to them, I discovered that I enjoy her more and more, and have now become friendly with them both. He has moved in with her and they plan to get married—after the divorce is final. She inherited a large house from her uncle, so they will be all set in terms of adequate space for the girls."

"And?" Celeste seemed bothered by all this news, coming as it did so thick and fast.

"And...that's all. I still live in our place, working at home, and I'm happy."

"Wow," was all Celeste could say.

"What news do you have for me?" Marcia asked. "Something must have happened in your life too."

"Well, I'm afraid I have a sadder story to tell you. First of all, I too have gotten a divorce. I've never loved John so much that I wanted to stay with him forever. Second, I was frustrated by my job, and I decided to quit. This was not a perfect solution, since it gets me more frustrated, and at loose ends. Since I didn't have children, life seems pretty empty—

emptier than it was before my divorce. That's my story in its totality."

After this conversation, Marcia and Celeste became better friends than ever. They never remarried and continued their small talk for years until they had nothing else to say. This lasted till they were too infirm to remember the last conversation, when they could start all over again.

GHOSTS

I was five years of age when my parents both died under mysterious circumstances. I was christened, as far as I know, Otis Bigelow. I was sent to my nearest relative, Esther, an aunt on my mother's side. She raised me as an only child because she wasn't married. She was very kind to me as a child, and because she had no children, she devoted herself to me with all her heart. She hoped to give me an excellent education, and began tutoring me at the age of five, when she came into my life. She could afford it, thanks to an inheritance from a distant relative, whom she barely knew. This was lucky for me since I had no hope of getting one otherwise. I learned quickly, and now consider myself, at the age of twenty-six, quite intelligent. One bit of training I retained from my childhood, despite my attempts to cure myself of it, was a belief in ghosts.

My aunt had many pictures of me and my father when he was about twenty-eight or twenty-nine years of age. This showed him clean-shaven as though he never had a beard. I remembered him from those days, an affectionate but distant father, and he always smelled of after-shave lotion. I thought of my fascination with ghosts, despite my age. I had taken up smoking at the time I was mature enough to do so, although, to be frank, I had experimented with smoking well before that. I had a clear vision of him at a later time. I was smoking at the time, and I blew a smoke ring, and it immediately condensed into an image of my father. He had a luxuriant beard! I thought

I was dreaming, but the act of my smoking, together with my tapping ash off my cigarette eliminated the idea. The beard was scraggled a bit, and he looked considerably older as if he had aged in death. But what did I know? I had heard of the Russian myth of bones and fingernails continuing to grow after death. Perhaps hair does the same thing. But my father was recognizable immediately.

Then a new apparition appeared to me. My mother appeared, framed by her hair, which had turned white like my father's beard. She had died many years ago about the time of my father's death. She introduced herself as Cora, my mother's first name. Despite her white hair and her aging countenance, I felt like I was talking to a ghost. I decided on a whim, to begin a conversation with her.

"So," I began, "it's been a long time since I saw you last! What have you been doing in the meantime? Needless to say, I'm surprised to see you: are you still living?"

"I'm not living, but hoping to confess the murder of your father to someone in the family. Since you're my only son, I hoped you would not predecease me." This astounded me.

"You murdered my father? I had no idea how he died. I thought he died of natural causes—a heart attack or something."

It was a surprisingly intimate conversation with my mother, all things considered. I wondered how my father had died so I asked my mother about the circumstances of his death. Was it violent, poison, or by a knife in an argument of some sort?

"I had a long-standing grudge against your father," she answered. "From the moment I married him, I knew it was a mistake. Because I worked as a nurse, I had access to various chemicals, and poisoned him with an overdose of morphine. I committed suicide before the authorities found out."

I thought about this for some time. By that time my mother—or her ghost—had disappeared, and I wondered whether this exchange with my mother or my mother's ghost was a dream after all. I couldn't believe how casual the conversation had been—she had confessed to my father's murder after—and I was astonished at her disposition. But had she just accomplished what she wanted, confessing to a crime followed by her suicide that covered her tracks? It seemed that she was relieved, and wanted no more of me.

I was anxious to seek confirmation from my father, but I couldn't find him no matter how much smoke I blew. He had died in his morphine-induced sleep and could not have answered anyway.

* * *

As I got older, I believed deeply in ghosts. I kept hearing something like mice in the walls, but couldn't figure out what the sounds actually were. They would often go away before I could identify them, but I was aware of them every day. Were these hordes of ghosts or simply the poor construction of the house? I decided on the latter, thinking that whatever they were it was easier to identify poor construction than ghosts. It was after I had taken all of the paneling off that it was clear it wasn't due to poor construction. It was something else. But I kept hearing the mice in the walls till my dying day.

I became a ghost once I had died of natural causes (old age, you'll be happy to know). I discovered that ectoplasm was quite flimsy stuff, and it would blow away if you weren't careful. It was as thin—thinner in fact—than cellophane. From the edge it is impossible to make out anyone's features, but full-on features like my father's beard and my mother's white hair were clear.

I was tempted to get the cellophane-like wrapping off me, and luckily I succeeded. That's how I died the second time, but now I can't figure out where I am anymore.

PARABLES

DOING GOD'S WORK

Olivia, a student of philosophy, worked hard at her chosen subject. She finally felt equipped to become a professional in the area. She was brought up as a strict Catholic, but she abandoned this early on (at the age of thirteen because 'it made no sense') in favor of philosophy. Her parents finally relented, knowing that Olivia was strong-willed, and had a mind of her own.

By the time she finished college, and after obtaining her Ph.D., she went on the market and secured a job at Yale University. She was very good at teaching from the very beginning, endowing her lectures with clarity, subtlety, and humor. She was promoted rapidly, achieving a professorial position after only six years.

Born to be a skeptic, Olivia was very beautiful. She had wavy brown hair, and penetrating brown eyes. She would ask the shrewdest questions of anyone that questioned *her*, to good effect. At an early age, she could hold her own in conversation, even with adults. This tended to make potential boyfriends shy away from her. At the age of thirty, she met a man, Dan, whose field was cosmology. They seemed to be made for one another. He was six years older than she was and, like her, was a skeptic, well-versed in clever argument. They would contend for hours at a time in good humor. He had a full professorship at Yale so that they didn't have to move very far to start living together. They married after she obtained her full professorship.

* * *

"Why did you go into philosophy?" Dan asked on a glorious spring day.

"Because I didn't know why people believed what they did," Olivia answered. "I thought I could get the answers from reading widely in the field. I've been fascinated and bitterly disappointed in my research on the subject. From Plato to Marx, I've never found an answer to the question of values, from politics to economics or anything else that makes any sense. But I keep on trying." Olivia took a deep breath before she continued. "Since my Catholic upbringing, I've been a troubled born-in-the-bone skeptic, which I don't regret for a moment."

"There must be some residual faith, but I can't figure out what it is," Dan answered. "I sense it in your attitude toward religion itself. It's as though you're trying to escape it, despite your rigid skepticism about it." Dan drew a deep breath himself.

Olivia answered by changing the subject. "Why did you go into cosmology? It seems as mysterious as religion itself. With the Big Bang Theory, which Fred Hoyle ridiculed in those exact terms, it seems truly ridiculous on its own."

"That's why they still call it a Theory—with a capital T—", Dan said with a smile. "I can't believe it myself unconditionally, but it's the best theory at the moment. There is no way of proving such a thing, and I don't believe it myself because it's a *theory*, not a fact. Most scientists believe that it is a singularity of nature, beyond which we don't know anything more. Some scientists believe that there are multiple universes. I haven't counted them, having lost count at 825." Dan waved his hand airily, thinking of it as a joke, which it was.

Olivia went back to the original subject. "As you well know, I'm working on a new book, for which I have a tentative title: *Evolution of Belief: A Darwinian Approach.* I hope it works. I am very hopeful that it will."

"Sounds interesting," said Dan, "are you still trying to exorcise the demons that haunt you so much?"

"A little bit," said Olivia, "I'm taking the perspective that the origin of belief itself is a singularity of nature, which I'm trying to figure out. When did it happen? Did it happen in the Neanderthals or later on? I can't find anything on the subject to work with. Did it arise before evolution was far advanced in *Homo sapiens*?" Dan and Olivia dropped the subject in favor of making love. She had never felt so much in love with Dan as she did that day.

* * *

After several years, Olivia finally published her book, which was greeted as a breakthrough and, in addition, a widely used textbook. Her relationship with Dan was going well, if routine. He was always pleasant and laid-back, whereas her activities took most of her time. She was, in other words, a thoroughly committed academic. She would come home in the afternoon or later, have a glass of wine and relax. She would make dinner for both of them, then go to her study and work there for several more hours.

Dan would occasionally drop in on her, and ask her what she was up to. He would ask, "What's cookin' good lookin'?" or some other banal phrase.

If she wasn't busy at the time, she would answer, "Nothing much, honey. Is there time for a last glass of wine before going to bed?"

"If you like, dear." They then went to bed, and embraced as they always did.

One night Dan spoke first, saying "Who, may I ask, appointed you as God, or his prophet? I've been wondering about this for some time."

Olivia answered, saying, "You have an impressive tolerance for ambiguity; I've noticed this since we first met."

"I just don't take things as seriously as you do," Dan said. "I noticed this too since the first time *we* first met. Don't worry about it. It adds spice to the marriage."

Olivia felt unsatisfied by this conversation, and considered a foreign trip or something else that would distract her. But she was so involved with the aftermath of her new book, that this was a passing thought, not a serious one. And so work and life went on.

Her curiosity drove her again to the subject of belief, since she was naturally curious about what the rest of the world thought. And so she rose in the ranks of academic philosophy, publishing frequently and becoming renowned as an expert in her studies. She read widely in the history and philosophy of science, and the combination made her an expert in both subjects. She found something interesting in the way people could believe in the 'damnedest things,' as she thought of it.

Dan and Olivia separated after a few more years. Olivia was tired of argument in the style to which they had become accustomed. Dan, on the other hand, remarried a woman who was much more compatible with him than Olivia. They corresponded for a time, but gradually this correspondence faded.

But, in the years following, Olivia began to have doubts about her own future, her natural skepticism growing on her day by day. She contemplated this skepticism which she had perfected over many years, and she decided it was futile. She thought of taking up psychology, but she already knew how flawed that field was. Again, she thought about the study of belief itself from a strictly scientific standpoint and how it could have developed in so many cultures. The question gnawed at her for a long time. Perhaps it never left her, even when she gave up her teaching and research entirely. She was close to retirement when she discovered aesthetics, a subject familiar to her from her youth as a Roman Catholic. Of course, she had been exposed to matters of aesthetics as they supported belief. Now, she could enjoy the works of the classical composers such as Haydn, Handel, and Mozart. The works of Bach were particularly attractive to her, as well as the unaccompanied compositions for cello. They were so deliberate and harmonious that she could not give up playing them over and over. She had never been interested in aesthetic pursuits per se before, but gradually her knowledge grew, in music especially, until she became a well-trained amateur in the subject and especially its beauty.

Realizing that life now had meaning, Olivia invested life with a glory she could fully enjoy.

ANATOMY OF A FAILURE

I'll be dead when you read this, but you can't say that I didn't try. I grew up quite well off, owing to my father's wealth. Until I was fifteen, life seemed to be a piece of cake, and everything came easily to me. I was fond of taking risks, and did so regularly. Like the time I went fishing on thin ice, which caved in because of my weight. I was becoming quite tall and heavy at the time, but hadn't realized it. The accident with the ice made me wary. A few years later I saw a man whipping a dog with his leash, and I turned him in to the police. I don't know what happened next, but I felt good about it.

Several years later, I came upon a crime in progress. It was an attempt to rob an ATM by dismantling it. (Some guys don't know how to operate an ATM, much less dismantle it.) I took the criminal in question to the police station, single-handedly—without a fight, no less. My imposing height and weight may have scared him, or he may simply have been too frustrated and exhausted to resist. I was pleased to see in the paper that he was charged with robbery, and due to the three strikes rule in effect at that time, he was sent to prison for thirty years.

My father died soon afterwards, leaving his estate to me. I was then thirty-four. There were no other heirs, since I was an only child. I decided to embark on a life of high risk, since this was a game I had played from childhood. It was thrilling to me, and since I was well off because of my father's estate, I could take chances. I was also smart, so I could be a daredevil freely and safely.

I thought to myself one day: why not go into a life of crime—just for fun, mind you? I was good at taking risks as I had found out during my childhood, except for the episode with the thin ice. So I felt that I could handle a life of crime without serious danger. Of course, there was a chance that I would be caught, but that added to the fun of it all.

This was a turning point, I knew. A life of crime made little sense, seeing as how I was wealthy (and handsome to boot). But I was looking for danger, some excitement in my life, something that would leave me with a sense of satisfaction. After trying some successful scams, I felt happy with my new career, and decided I would continue to pursue it. Then I was caught. I attempted to steal money from an ATM. You remember the occasion when I caught a poor fellow dismantling an ATM? He got a thirty year sentence, which I could not afford since it would deprive me of leading the exciting life I desired. Thankfully my lawyers got me off with a mere six months, because I didn't have prior convictions and promised to pay back the money. This left me with a residual sense of shame, which never left me. I had failed this time, and so I promised myself never to take risks again. This left me without a sense of purpose, which I missed greatly—so greatly, in fact, that occasionally I contemplated suicide.

This was another turning point. I kept contemplating how to harm myself without breaking the law. For instance, I thought it would be inventive, as it had been in the past, to avoid paying taxes on my father's estate by finding an offshore account of some sort. This was not breaking the law, it turned out, and so it lacked the satisfaction I enjoyed. Another example occurred to me: I could stop paying taxes altogether by not submitting my 1040 form or at least underestimate my taxes. This was breaking the law, as I was aware, and as my lawyers told me in no uncertain terms. They were used to seeing my risk-taking behavior at this point, so they had become wary about my doings. This was a ridiculous idea, I finally conceded, and another failure.

I became bored with life and didn't know what to do about this. Everything seemed just blah to me, and I once again considered suicide, this time more seriously. The prospect of causing myself pain did not appeal to me. But I heard of the use of OxyContin mixed with yogurt to commit suicide in relative comfort, and I tried this as my means of doing the job. It was a moment of impulse, I agree, but I was assured by the literature on the subject that it would be effective.

Surprisingly, I awoke from this attempt, logy but oddly refreshed (after the medical team had revived me). I realized that this attempt at suicide had also been a failure, as most of my attempts at pleasure had been in the recent past.

I am now 90 years of age, still healthy, still bored to tears with my life, and still waiting for the end, which will happen any day. I hope that my wait won't be in vain.

ENVY

Friends (of whom I have few) tell me that I was a foundling, left on the steps of the Ebenezer Baptist Church by my parents, because I didn't grow. I was baptized by the church as Cecil Little since I was so small. I don't know who found me, but I was brought up in the church as a 'sad case' until I was twelve. In the meantime, I was taught to read and write by the kindness of the pastor of the church and his wife, who regarded me as something of a pet. By the time I was mature (or as mature as I was going to get), it was 1860. I was fortunate to be trained in reading and writing, since I cannot have learned these skills otherwise. Then it seemed, because of limited resources, in the best interest of the church to let me go my own way. This seemed cruel even to me, having worked for the church for my whole life. I was asked to do menial tasks around the church such as setting up meals for the pastor and cleaning toilets. By the time the church disposed of me, I weighed almost thirty pounds. I learned this from a free pay scale, near the church after the church let me go. I was hunched and hobbled, finding it hard to walk.

From then on life was difficult—more difficult than you can imagine. I tried to find employment, but because of my size, I found nothing suitable for my talents (which I thought were considerable). I was helped in the interim by strangers who looked on my fate as tragic. After a series of menial jobs including one once again cleaning restrooms, my talents at reading and writing were recognized by a newspaper, and I was employed once more.

At the newspaper, I was given the job of correcting the editorial errors, of which there were a number. I was able to work despite the height of the stool, because ladder-like rungs holding the legs of the stool apart allowed me to climb up to the broad table, where I could work easily. This table was broad so that I could open the paper to its full width. Eventually the newspaper found it easier to put a large board on the floor where I could work. I could proofread happily from that time on.

Shortly the war between the states began. I didn't know what to do, since the newspaper office was burned down, and I was unemployed again. I decided right then and there that I could sign up for duty with the Confederate side, if it would have me. Because of a lack of manpower they took me readily, and they would decide what to do with me later. They finally fitted me out in child-size heavy boots, and a small uniform of sorts with a badge of the Confederacy taken from a dead soldier. They enrolled me in the 9th Division of the regular army, where I could be of use as a general handyman. From then on I could be useful in jobs ranging from toilet cleaning (a natural skill by now) to writing dispatches to the front. All in all, it was a satisfying life as long as I stayed out of danger. When I felt danger near, I felt my small size would protect me from harm.

As a hunched and hobbled man, much too small for combat, I stood aside as the battles raged. I later roamed among the brave and broken bodies, collapsed in their uniforms. I looked into the eyes of the mortally wounded and for the first time saw envy, pure envy.

I DREAM, THEREFORE I AM

Victor, a graduate student, ever curious about the field of psychology, was mentored by his professor, newly hired from Columbia University. The professor's name was Hugh Levins. Levins was only a few years older than Victor, having been hired as an assistant professor. Levins suggested that they collaborate in a curious experiment. Victor would 'lend his mind' to Levins in hopes that the latter could control his dreams. He was promised publication rights on the paper, if it were accepted for publication. Victor was a new student at the University of Wisconsin and thus a bit naïve, so he enthusiastically accepted the deal.

"Excellent," said Levins, "I see you are daring, and are willing to indulge me in what I think is an exciting experiment."

"Glad to be of use," Victor replied, "anything you want. Your whim is my command."

In a dimly lit room, preparations for the experiment began. At first, the only sedation to induce sleep consisted of dimming the lights. Victor was nevertheless excited. It was practice for the main event, which would follow in a week or so. It was good practice, because by that time Victor could relax easily once he had lain down. The next week, Levins attached electrodes to Victor's head, and the experiment began. At first he felt strangely comfortable with the process, and was surprised that he fell asleep almost immediately. But soon he realized that he remembered nothing about the dream he had, not the content or even the mood it left him in. Victor was strangely disturbed by this. When he asked Levins about this, Levins was surprised and worried that the experiment might be a failure. They would try again the next week.

Victor remained committed to the experiment, hoping for success this time. The prospect of publication was still high in his mind. Indeed, since this was an original experiment it could be a landmark. Levins had assured him that the experiment *was* important, and his explanation of the details and the nature of the investigation convinced Victor to stay on.

Victor spent the next week worrying about what would happen if the experiment failed again. Levins kept reassuring him by saying that experiments took time to perfect and not to worry about initial failures. And so together they tried not to worry about failures, but simply went about their business. After a number of further failures they got used to them. Then suddenly they had success when Victor was rewarded by remembering his dream in detail. The dream itself was disturbing because it reflected a terrible accident he experienced when he was a child. The car he was riding in overturned, and his parents were terribly hurt but survived. Victor had apparently suppressed the memory and not thought about the incident in years. By the time of the experiments, he had effectively forgotten. The fact that he could now remember a long-buried memory so vividly in a dream was quite disturbing. The next night Victor awoke in the same cot, having retrieved a similar long forgotten childhood memory in his dream. Levins was very excited and poured two glasses of champagne to celebrate their success.

Things thereafter proceeded according to plan, but since Victor was taking time from his studies he was increasingly anxious. He asked for time off, but Levins was so excited by their progress that he was reluctant to agree. So they went on with the experiments having one success after another. They couldn't stop when it was going so well, so Levins offered to hire Victor as a part-time assistant. Victor readily agreed.

All was fine as long as it was a matter of simply retrieving lost memories, but then things took an ugly turn. Victor felt that memories were being imposed on him. Victor had the feeling that they were original, not long-buried ones he could report in detail, and they faded quickly, like ordinary dreams. When he asked Levins what was going on, Levins was elusive about the nature of the current experiments. Victor threatened to quit the job, having lost faith in Levins He did so after a few more trials.

With these troubling thoughts behind him, Victor felt free to go on with his life.

* * *

I awoke in the same familiar cot in the dimly lit room, having trouble distinguishing Victor and Alex, my given name. What had Levins done? Had he succeeded in giving me a new personality? The new dreams he had given me, especially those of my future, were especially difficult to accept. When fully awakened, I confronted Levins, and threatened to quit as I had in the previous dream. I walked out into the sunlight, under the elms, still troubled by the confusion that assaulted me, and which still confuses me occasionally, in my waking hours.

After this, learning, love, and life went on, for what seemed like a very long time, years. I had met a wonderful girl in the dining room of my dormitory with whom I developed an intimate relationship. My studies continued to be successful to the point where I received a prestigious fellowship in my new field, biology. I worried less about the dreams I had had under the guidance of Levins, but wondered still if I were Alex, or my dream counterpart, Victor. These thoughts became less troubling with time and gradually I forgot them. It was no time for obsession, I told myself, since I was spending a great deal more time with Jenna, my girlfriend.

One fine sunny day, Alex awoke in an all too familiar cot. I had not aged at all. Levins was standing by, and said, "Victor, it seems to have worked! I could hear you breathing regularly and see you remming furiously for a long time. What do you remember?" (Remming was shorthand for 'rapid eye movements' characteristic of the onset of dreams.).

Alex answered, aghast, "What has happened to me? I live my life for several years, and I wake up in this damned cot again! Have you implanted a new personality on me? You called me Victor!"

Levins for the first time understood the dangers of his experiments. He was deeply troubled. "I'm so sorry the experiments have produced a crisis in your thoughts about your identity. What can I do to help?"

"Nothing." Alex was furious. "Maybe you could return me to the dream so I can get on with my life," he said sarcastically.

"I'm afraid I can't do that," Levins said somberly, "I know how to start them, but not how to continue them or conclude them" Levins said in a more hopeful tone, "Will you still be my co-author?"

"No," Alex—or was it Victor—said in confusion, "I'm out of here." He turned on his heel and left the building.

As he strode into the morning light among the elms, he knew he would never know whether he was awake. Jenna was gone with the dream, and years later, after a life without meaning, he tested his existence, on impulse, by stepping into traffic. As he fell beneath the wheels, he was almost certain he would not awaken, ever again.

GOD LEARNS FROM THE PRIEST

The high priest had contemplated creation for a lifetime. Its magnificence called for a creator, but his belief was tested by the silence of God. He had worried for decades that his faith would fail. As he neared death, he retired and concentrated harder, hoping to have a vision or a word from beyond the earth. One sunlit day he heard a voice audible only to him. The creator wished to speak with him. Nothing was visible but the familiar sky, the sun, and the fertile plain below his retreat.

The creator said, "You are an interesting fellow. I have been following your thoughts, curious about your understanding of your world. I myself have much to learn about my creation."

The high priest answered, his mind ablaze, "I feel privileged beyond measure to speak to you. Surely you know everything, far more that I do. Have you spoken to others?"

"Not one, though I have explored the minds of many. You're the first to whom I felt I could speak. As recently as one of your years ago, I didn't know this planet existed."

"*What?*" said the priest. "You did not know about us?"

"No, but I have learned much since I found my way here. Why do you ask?"

"Are you not God, ruler of the heavens and our fountain of goodness? I...I really don't understand. Are you just a visitor from another world? Where did you come from? What do you wish from us? From me?"

"You could call me God, if you like the word. But you are misled if you think I have been here before now. I am sorry if I bothered you. I certainly don't want anything from you. I am simply interested, and I really have nothing to give."

"Where did you come from?" The priest's voice trembled.

"I came to be by an act of will, if you can understand that. I suppose you don't, but it must be like one of your kind awaking with ambition but no memory. No...no, that's not right. I could hardly hope to explain it. But by the same means I brought into existence what you see around you."

"Everything?"

"Yes, everything you can see with your most powerful devices. And much more."

"So you are the Creator of all things? Am I really speaking to God?"

"Yes, I suppose that's true, but don't take me too seriously. I made a huge mistake, which led to many more mistakes. I had hoped to create a splendid, perfect harmony, all energy and glorious light, huge and smooth, growing without end. That appealed to me. The universe enlarged beautifully at first, as I planned. But suddenly it began to clot and formed the mess you see now. I hope to succeed next time."

"Next time?" The priest was aghast. "When would that be?"

"Soon. But before that, I will try to understand what went wrong. All this matter, as you call it, this coagulated material. Since I have been listening to you and your kind, I literally don't know what the matter is, as you sometimes put it. You would call that a play on words, if I am not mistaken. I never thought my creation would condense like that. Everything is random, colliding, burning, out of control."

"You aren't the God we've worshipped all these years. Where is he? Something, some entity that brought *us* into existence and endows us with hope for good and with a knowledge of evil."

"You go beyond my familiarity with your world, the most unusual I have encountered. You must understand that I was not aware of your existence, and would not be still if some coherent, complicated activities and thoughts emanating from your planet did not draw me here. In addition to the signals and inert matter of your planet, I saw a chaos of forms, many moving about, growing and multiplying. Their variety disturbed me, but I could see in each a systematic beauty. You call this life, I believe. But I don't know the words good and evil that you mentioned."

The priest thought for some time. "I am either deluded or you really are God or I am speaking to an extraterrestrial being."

"Indeed, I am not of your world, and I am the creator of the universe. But you cannot possibly know much about me. In fact, you seem to have filled your ignorance with unusual and untrue pictures and ideas. On my part, I am almost as ignorant as you are about the universe, because it was a huge mistake. In fact, you may have discovered something that you call God, but I might not recognize it if I encountered it. Nor, perhaps, would you. Perhaps later you can tell me more about it so I can watch for it.

The priest looked confused. "But how did you make *us*? We are hardly just clots of matter."

"From what I've seen, you must be wrong. You are part of the matter that appeared soon after the explosion. Your world has many strange and wonderful things, like yourself. I did not know you existed until recently. You and all the living things around you arose without my planning or intervention. I would not know how to intervene if I tried. It is an outgrowth of the matter that formed in error. All I can change are the big things, like rates and compression and distances, all at once. Nothing on a small scale."

"How do you know that God—our God, at least—was not created, also a result of your mistake, and he went on to create us?"

"I haven't sensed any other being, and I think I would have noticed. I noticed you, after all, and surely you are a very small part of what your so-called God made. Your God, if he exists, must be gone now. In fact, I cannot imagine his leaving you if he existed. Or if he remained interested."

"But He *is* here, he must be," the priest insisted.

"What makes you think so?"

"Doesn't it make sense to you? You regret the mistakes you made, but we and the living world certainly couldn't be mistakes!"

"All I can say is that anything is possible."

"I confess," said the priest, "that some of us think exactly that. But I simply don't believe it. Our scientists say that living things were not always this way, what you see now. They say that complicated chemicals formed spontaneously, and some found a way to grow and duplicate. I don't know how, perhaps even the scientists don't. I am sure they don't. But these chemicals made mistakes and some mistakes made them better, not worse. More and more of the better ones formed, getting even better and more complicated all the time. These scientists say…"

"Amazing!" the creator exclaimed. "I see it immediately. I would never have predicted that! Of course, I never predicted my original mistake. I never saw anything that behaves the way you describe, and I have visited many places. Perhaps you will tell me more about it later. But the idea is so simple I might have imagined it after all, even if I had not visited you here. It tempts me to let this mistake continue, simply to see what new things form. All I can do is watch the details. Or I can begin again. It has already changed my plans for the next time. Let matter form after all, and make better use of it. A little more control at the outset."

The creator became impatient. "For now," he said to the priest, "I must leave you to think, as you say. I have much to think about and to do."

The high priest widened his eyes, feeling an empty silence close around him. He breathed deeply and shook his head. I now wish to die, he thought, before my faith is wrenched from me entirely. The creator I spoke with has a distant wonder at our world. But he—why "he?"—is not our God. He was quick of mind, powerful, clumsy. He made mistakes and failed to predict life itself. Our own God shaped the mistakes and gave us a destiny that cannot be a property of matter. It simply can't be. As the high priest nodded and leaned into the realm of the dead, he knew that the silence he had heard all his life was real after all.

The creator, still contemplating the results of his experiment, erased the bungled universe and started again, this time aware that energy would condense and matter would appear. By careful adjustment of the beginnings, the creator felt he could refine the properties of matter and impel it to form life that would multiply sooner, more readily, more wonderfully.

But living things such as those the creator had seen on the priest's planet never appeared in the second universe, or the third universe or the many other universes he made.

Pity.

ALONE

Kayama heard that after the Great Wave the dead tried to be heard in dreams of survivors, with voices urging caution, intoning warnings too late to matter. Now after ten thousand suns only the very young and the very old could hear their forebears. Children would awaken with disquiet, unable to remember, unable to tell their friends and parents of their dreams. Those about to die sometimes warned the people about what they had learned in their sleep, but no one believed them. Kayama, the sun child, soon to lead the tribe, urged his people to listen, to ask their children what they knew, why they were disturbed, what the dead had told them. The tribe now thrived on their undiscovered island in the new growth of palms and casuarina, of breadfruits and berry-bearing vines. The gods gave them cod and flying fish and sharks and crabs and shellfish, an ocean of food and wonder.

Kayama heard voices in the whipping of the palms and the sighs of the casuarina as they bent and swished in the wind, in the talk of kookaburras and magpies as they gathered in the eucalyptus. He sensed in the roots of the breadfruit trees stealing under his hut a subtle threat he could not understand. Snakes would writhe before him, whipping their tails like signals as he entered the damp inland forest. His woman Alima told him in her calm voice to smile, to be without fear, to let dreams be forgotten and signs be ignored. She said their people were joyous now and multiplying, haunted only by the dim memory of the Great Wave and troubled dreams.

But three years after their child Moroca was born, she would not sleep, she would not rest, she dreaded the dark. She tried to tell Alima of visitors in the night, of people she did not know, people who vanished as she woke, people who spoke of the future. Moroca knew of the Wave before Alima or Kayama told her the story. Moroca gave fearful shape to similar dreams in her young friends, and Alima had to keep Moroca away from them.

The elders spoke warnings too, of a Wave yet to come. They urged Kayama to gather the people away from the shore. Weeks later, the earth spoke to Kayama in a low voice that shook the ground. The sea deserted the shore and left fish and seaweed behind, and the gulls and terns gathered in multitudes to feed on the life left on the seabed. Kayama called for all to come to the center, not out toward the receding ocean. Many failed to heed him, and the sea returned in a towering wave that swept away all but those in the center of the island. Kayama and his survivors, even in their exhaustion, slept poorly, sadly, clustered for many weeks in the jungled center. They feared their gods now, gods of the sea, gods of great waves, gods that could not be trusted. The tribe even feared the sea lapping steadily at the jumbled coral and bare lava of the shore.

And the dead awakened again in the dreams of the survivors, sad, repentant, and again warned of storms and waves. Old men and women told of visits in the night from their sons and daughters, already gone. And children spoke of rats and snakes, rats coming to molest them, to eat their fingers in their sleep. All the remaining people and animals were hungry and fertile and the remaining land could not feed them. Kayama, their leader, could not convince his people to be brave, to stay in the center, to now ignore signs and dreams if they could.

A storm came to the island, with winds and high seas, and it cleaned the sparse beaches, took all the sand, leaving only lava and stones. The ebb tide left a dead, bearded man with white skin and ragged jeans on the rattling rocks of the shore. The men and women of the tribe gathered, staring in wonder at the strange body. Soon, a deeper loneliness stole into their hearts as they realized they were no longer alone.

CPSIA information can be obtained at www.ICGtesting.com
Printed in the USA
LVOW05s2023130913

352214LV00001B/61/P